After discovering the General has taken her mother into hiding, Cameo relies on Rebar's tracking device and unexpected help to plan a rescue mission. She's intrigued by the hunky bikers who come to their aid.

Not all goes as planned during the rescue. Two of their team members get left behind and one makes a narrow escape. The General and his daughters prove yet again that they are a force to be reckoned with.

When everything goes sideways, everyone ends up in the wrong place, leaving Rebar wondering about the future with his new girlfriend.

Her Secret Weapon
Copyright © 2023 Shiloh Love
ISBN: 978-1-4874-4047-3
Cover art by Martine Jardin

Published by eXtasy Books Inc

Look for us online at:
www.eXtasybooks.com

HER SECRET WEAPON
FEATHER BLUE: 4

BY

SHILOH LOVE

CHAPTER ONE

"Baby, you've got to tell me more about your new invention," Cameo said as she and Rebar enjoyed a late-night meal of his special Ramen dish. "I saw you swipe your palms before you shook Joan's hand. It was a smooth move, very discreet. How do you keep it from absorbing into your skin? Will you show the gadget to me? And I'm still wondering how you managed to give it to both of them, and how you had the two devices inside your hand."

"I shook their hands, remember? And I was fast. You were probably too distraught to notice me reach into my pocket. I did it all super-fast."

"You're a genius. Now show me how we can see if the devices are working?"

A flattered smile touched his ruggedly handsome face, which bore a heavy evening shadow after their long day of road-tripping.

"Sure, I will. First, I need to pull up the app on my computer to check the status and see if it's working. We should be able to follow their every move. The thermal tracking is amalgamated into zinc and protected by emollients that instantly absorb upon contact with the host."

"Sounds complex."

"Very. I've been working on this one for years. *Eye Candy* was a bit easier to design because it's an actual metal device that's swallowed in pill form. The biggest issue I had with *Face Palm* was keeping the tracking components intact long enough to get into a host."

"And how do you do that? Don't they go into *your* skin before you transfer it to your target?"

"They did at first. But I found a good binder that doesn't soak through rice paper too quickly. Once contact is made, the other person may feel a bit of moisture or stickiness but not so much as they'd think anything of it. And by the time they reach for the hand sanitizer or wash their hands, the tracking device is already in their system."

"Rice paper?" She blinked in surprise. "Fascinating."

"It's practically weightless, translucent and dissolves instantly when combined with my emollient mixture. Just a small square, about the size of a postage stamp will do the job."

"How'd you come up with the idea?"

"Once I invented Eye Candy, it was just a matter of playing around with variations of the thermal device I'd already devised. I found a way to melt Eye Candy into a dissolvable medium. Took some doing but I figured it out."

She rested her chin on both hands, gazing at him with utter adoration. How she loved watching his mind in action. So much intelligence was undeniably appealing. "Is this new invention patented yet?"

"Patent pending," he replied. "I sold Eye Candy. I'm sure this new tracking system will bring heavy bidders. Can you imagine what the military could do with this? Eye Candy must be swallowed. Face Palm can be attached to any intended live target. The possibilities are endless. I just need to check for glitches. Today was the first time I decided to actually put it to the test. I need to know exactly how long it remains active once released into a host. Once I have that down, I can sell it."

"I'm bursting with curiosity. Let's go see if it's working." Cameo was beyond impressed by her genius boyfriend. Not only was he brilliant but gorgeous, too. Some days she had to pinch herself to make sure she wasn't imagining he was her man.

"Are you finished eating?" he asked, peeking into her bowl. "Do you want more? We had a long, daunting day."

"I'm stuffed. I really want to see your invention and see if it's working. If we can track Missy and Joan, we may find my mother before the General does something even more insane."

His expression brightened with enthusiasm, indicating he also was anxious to know if his brainchild was a success. They set their empty dishes in the sink then walked into his den. She looked around at the numerous devices and gadgets on his desk and utilities tables. Cords running everywhere were plugged into surge protectors then into wall outlets. This was the one area of his home that wasn't pinpoint neat.

"First time I've been in this room," she said, gawking around at all the technical equipment.

"Sorry it's a mess." He straightened a stack of papers on a giant rolltop desk. "Nobody comes in here except me . . . until now." He pulled an extra chair up to his desk and gestured for her to have a seat.

She sat beside him and watched absorbedly as he booted up a high-end computer. He entered codes and passwords on several devices to access a screen of grids.

"What am I looking at?" she asked, totally lost.

"Maps." He leaned forward and studied the screen. "If the device activated properly, I should see activity somewhere." He looked from screen to screen, tapping various keys and functions. "There!" He pointed to a tiny purple blip. "It's working! Hot damn!" Then he fingered another blip. "There's the other one. Bingo. Both chicks on radar." He looked up at her excitedly.

Cameo couldn't resist giving him a warm kiss to share his success. She watched the blips move just slightly. "Where are they?"

He checked a readout coming through on another device. "They haven't left the house. I'll set the alert so we can get some sleep. I have a feeling they'll make their move sometime tomorrow."

"That doesn't give us much time to tell the troop what happened." She worried about going in by themselves again.

"We can't head out until we know their heading. Who knows where the General has taken your mother? We just gotta sit back and be patient. No need to follow Missy and Joan. Once they reach their destination, we'll have the address and can move in." He leaned back in his chair, arms folded behind his neck.

"What's wrong?" She sensed him pondering something.

"I'm not sure if we should tell the troop about Face Palm yet."

"You're worried someone will tip them off?"

He made direct eye contact with her. "How'd you know that's what I was thinking?"

"I had the same thought when we got down there and found out the General had taken Malika away, and by the looks of things it was a rushed exit." Cameo rolled her mother's gold earring around in her palm, the earring found near the General's mansion door.

"We'll find her. I have a phone synced with this computer. I'll keep it by the bed with the volume up. If they start to move beyond a five-mile radius the alert will sound."

She pondered everything, awed by his speed of thought. "I wonder if the old man adheres to the 'keep your enemies closer' theory or if he'll go completely opposite and leave the country."

"He'd never leave the States," Rebar said. "All his power and friends are here. And I doubt he'll go too far from those girls of his. He's no spring chicken and Malika is a handful.

I'm guessing his villa is within a hundred miles of his home." He pulled her onto his lap. "Don't waste energy trying to guess his next move. You need sleep and calm thoughts."

"You're right." She snuggled against him. He smelled good, like leather, fresh wood, and a hint of patchouli. His black-brown, freshly washed hair had grown a couple of inches and hung in damp strands just past his collar. She basked in the comfort of his strength and unique allure.

Cameo woke to the aroma of bacon wafting through the house. She yawned, stretched, and looked around. Rebar must've carried her up to bed when she'd fallen asleep in his lap last night. They'd had an exhausting day, both mentally and physically. She marveled at his stamina, to be up already cooking breakfast. Her man seemed to need minimal sleep to thrive.

She dragged herself out of his luxurious bed and to the master bath mirror. Her long hair was a tangled mess. She hadn't brushed it after showering and before falling asleep. She began working the tangles out with a pin brush while looking at her reflection.

I am too thin, she thought. Both Shade and Rebar had mentioned it. She turned to one side, then the other. *Well, it's not like I don't eat.* She stared at her reflection, then applied eye makeup to accent her blue eyes. Her long blonde hair hung to her waist, which pleased her. The mams at her last boarding school forbade girls from cutting their hair. And when Malika found her in London, she expressed joy over Cameo's 'diva splendor' as her mother had fondly remarked.

Diva. Cameo scoffed. *Hardly.* But she didn't fault Malika for her vanity. Her mother was denied all contact with her twins. She had barely begun to get acquainted with her mother before the General took Malika away. Cameo longed to show her mother that there was so much more to her than outward beauty. She carried a black belt in Karate, had several degrees in science and an impressive resume. She wondered if Malika knew anything at all about her.

She pulled on a pair of shorts, then a tank top, before heading downstairs. Sitting on the edge of the bed, she pulled her thoughts together and tried to be more awake before greeting her sweet loving man.

Lately, she'd been spending more nights in Rebar's bed than her own. She loved his lodge, as he affectionately called it. It was much roomier than her loft apartment and he was very clean and neat. She also liked the fact that he was very private.

Still, she wondered if she should spend more time in her own place so maybe Rebar's friends would come around, most notably Chamber. She got the impression when they'd met that Chamber was staying away because of her. And she definitely didn't want to drive his friends away. Her connection to Malika had placed a huge wall between her and Rebar's friends.

But she couldn't consciously leave her mother in the General's clutches. She knew better than anyone what that beast was capable of. Cameo was determined to rescue Malika from the tyrant.

She decided the best approach would be to come straight out and speak with Rebar about her concerns. Surely, he'd be honest with her if she was cramping his space. She padded down the stairway barefooted and found him in the dining room, wearing only a pair of faded jeans while plating their breakfast.

"Bacon and eggs?" She was surprised as they usually ate breakfast cakes and fruit.

He looked up with a dazzling smile. "Every now and then I do the hearty country breakfast thing."

"Everything looks and smells delicious." She slid onto a

chair at the table. "Did you even sleep?"

"I got a few hours. Did you sleep well?" He sat across from her.

"I always sleep good here." She smiled. "Do you think I'm spending too many nights here? Maybe I should start sleeping at my place more."

"Why do you ask?" Disappointment shadowed his face.

"Well . . . Chamber has not yet come to stay. I don't want to be in the way."

"Ah babydoll, you could never be in the way. The guys have a lot to process. I'm sure Jackson and Shade are doing their best to keep everyone loyal to the General. Tension is running high with the bomb we dropped on them. They know it's the truth. You had photos to back it up. Smart move on your part."

She shrugged modestly. "Just one of those split-second decisions. Although Shade accused me of photoshopping."

"Don't pay attention to that. I think it was the shock of seeing the photo. I enjoy your company very much. But I don't want you to feel pressured either. If you need time to yourself, I understand. Don't stop staying for the wrong reasons."

"Okay. I'll give it more thought." She gazed at him dreamily. "By the way, you look sexier than ever this morning."

A grin touched his lips. "I feel more comfortable around you. This is what I usually wear around the house."

"You can wear less anytime you want," she teased.

"Not while I'm here," a man's voice said lightly from the other room. "I don't need to see all that."

Cameo swung around to see Chamber strolling into the kitchen. Faded jeans covered his long legs, and he wore combat boots and a black sleeveless tee. Layered blond hair fell recklessly in long pointcut strands around his face. His gaze went straight to her. Those unforgettable green eyes made solid contact with hers.

"Hey, Cameo," he said warmly. "Nice to see you again."

"Nice to see you, too." She offered him a friendly smile. "I was beginning to worry my presence here was scaring Rebar's friends away."

He pulled up a chair and plopped down beside her. "A pretty little thing like you scare us away? Nah. Rebar's true friends are smart enough to trust his judgment in who he keeps company with."

Rebar got up and grabbed another plate then slid it over to Chamber. "You're just in time for breakfast, mate."

"You're eating bacon?" Chamber laughed. "What's the occasion?"

"Shut up." Rebar laughed and playfully flipped him off.

Chamber laughed with him. He had a beautiful smile that revealed perfect white teeth. He and Rebar were by far the handsomest men of the troop, despite how Malika had gushed over Shade.

"I'm the only one who knows about Rebar's flair for Ramen," Chamber told her with a wink.

"Me, too, now. He does make good Ramen," she said.

"Ah, so he's let you in on his secrets."

"Yes." She smiled at Rebar. "I seemed to have earned his trust and likewise."

"Glad to hear it." Chamber forked a bite of scrambled eggs into his mouth then munched down some bacon.

"What's the status with the troop?" Rebar asked. "Cameo and I drove down to the General's house yesterday. There are more shocking developments."

Chamber finished chewing, then swallowed a few gulps of juice before speaking. "Some are still on the fence. Jackson and Shade don't want to be involved because of Camille's feelings on the matter.

"I assume you've made your decision. You're here."

"You had doubts?" Chamber slanted him a wounded look.

"A little," admitted Rebar. "This is an unusual situation."

"Yeah," Chamber said with a light laugh. "That's putting it mildly. But you should've known I'd never bail on you. And the two of you should've called me before going down to the General's house without backup. With Joan and Malika on the loose, the General acting strangely . . . anything could've happened."

"It got tense, and we didn't know we'd find them there," Rebar admitted. "So tell me, what's your take on the troop? Tell me straight up."

"Not good," replied Chamber between bites. He seemed hungry. "Talon and Kohl want to join us because of their connection to your unmatchable techno skills. But Shade's laying on the heat. He told the guys if they help Malika in anyway, they can consider themselves permanently dismissed from the troop."

Rebar continued eating, not saying anything straight off as he seemingly pondered everything. Cameo remained quiet, observing the two men, and respecting their need to sort matters. The three of them finished breakfast in calm silence. She didn't feel awkward, though. She could tell they had a lot on their minds.

"I'll clear the table," she told them once everyone had finished.

Rebar slanted her a questioning look then nodded his thanks. "We'll help. You're not a maid. Then we'll head into the den. I want to show Chamber something."

She smiled knowingly and was happy that her presence hadn't created distrust between Rebar and his best friend. She felt bad enough over the dissension with Shade, Jackson, and Camille. Hopefully, her twin would want to reconcile one day. Perhaps once she realized that their mother was not the one to blame for their separation at birth she would come to her senses.

"Lost in thought?" Rebar tenderly gathered her hair to one side while making eye contact.

"A little." She smiled. "A lot on my mind."

"I can imagine." He took her hand. "C'mon. Let's show Chamber my new baby."

Chamber gave Rebar an intrigued look. "Get a new car?"

"Nope." Rebar led them to his workspace and chuckled. "Although that would be awesome, too, but I'd hardly be keeping that in the den. But no, I've been working on something. Haven't shown it to anyone except Cameo."

"Ah, she *has* earned your trust. Must be a very special lady." He gave Cameo a wink.

Rebar pulled two extra chairs up to his desk. "Have a seat."

Chamber politely waited for her to sit before he plopped onto the other chair. They scooted up close as Rebar booted up his system.

"I've been working on this since the launch of Eye Candy," he told Chamber. "I've taken tracking to the outer limits."

Cameo quietly observed and listened as Rebar showed Chamber the graphs and explained the logistics of Face Palm.

"Damn . . ." Chamber let out a sigh. "You're like the next William James Sidis or something. How'd you put this one together?"

"Who's that?" Cameo asked.

"Smartest man in history," Chamber replied. Then he gave her a wink. "So far."

Rebar smiled modestly. "I spent a lot of time alone the past several years. If I don't put my brain to work, it'll come up with things to do on its own that aren't generally good."

Chamber laid a hand on his friend's shoulder. "I know, man. Your battle with PTSD has been tough. I admire your effort to adapt and overcome it without drugs or alcohol."

"Is that the connection you have with Camille?" Her question tumbled out before she could stop it. She pursed her lips together regretfully then added, "Sorry." But the thought remained. She had a hard time forgetting the way he'd gazed at her when they first met and he'd thought she was Camille.

"No, it's okay," Rebar soothed. "And yeah, that *was* the connection I had with her. She's different now. Or maybe I am. Either way, Camille and I no longer have a connection or share similar viewpoints. Her petulance over Malika, and her manipulation tactics, don't sit well with me at all."

"I'm sorry you suffer with PTSD."

His expression softened as he stared at her with those hauntingly dark eyes. "Thanks, babydoll."

"If you ever need to talk, I'm a good listener."

"Someday I'll tell you about it," he said with a grateful smile. Then he turned toward Chamber. "I'm in the process of running the first live test of this one. I slipped it onto Joan and Missy before the fight."

"Fight?" Chamber's brows arched.

Rebar laughed a little. "Once we realized Malika wasn't there, those two whack-jobs tried to stop us from leaving." He paused for a moment, then added, "Bet you didn't know Cameo holds a black belt."

"Really?" Chamber looked even more surprised.

"We kicked ass. Left the two wenches in a heap on the floor, then split. Actually, Cameo kicked ass. I held Missy back while she took care of Joan. You know, to even the odds. Though, after watching her in action, I think she could've taken them both at the same time."

Chamber shifted his focus to Cameo. "Skinny girl like you thumped Missy and Joan? Missy has combat training."

"So it seems," Cameo said with a slight grin. "Too bad her skills don't match her ego."

"Where'd you get a black belt?"

"I hired a private instructor while in boarding school and continued training afterward. Though the General shipped

11

me off when I was five, he did send an allowance. Instead of using it on frivolous things, I used it to protect myself from bullies. Skinny girls from out-of-town look like easy targets. After I won my first fight, nobody picked on me again."

"I'm impressed. Do you know Rebar also holds a black belt?"

"I didn't know that. But I'm not surprised. I imagine he is quite skilled in the art of combat being a Marine and all."

"Don't take this the wrong way, but I wish I could've watched you take those two bitches down," Chamber said with a grin.

"I get it." She laughed lightly. "Men love chic fights."

Chamber shrugged, still wearing a silly grin. "What can I say? I'm a guy."

"No worries."

He gazed at her for several moments as if scrutinizing her inside and out. Those intense green eyes seemed to stare straight through her. She had nothing to hide and didn't look away.

"Ya know, darlin'," Chamber began. "Though you are identical in appearance to Camille, you carry a completely different aura. There's something about you that sets you apart from her. I'll have no trouble telling the two of you apart if we're ever all together again."

She let out a sigh. "That's a big if. The way things look now, I don't expect to reconnect with my sister anytime soon. Sad that she's so jaded. It's not our mother's fault that we were separated at birth."

"Seems Jared and the General accomplished what they set out to do," Chamber said with visible sadness in his eyes.

"Yes." She agreed. "And now at least one of them is going to pay. Mother had a plan. She didn't reveal the details, but she definitely made it known that he would be held accountable. Unfortunately, they must've blindsided her before she got to carry it out. I'm not sure she knew Joan was still alive. Everything is very murky."

"We were all stunned to find out Joan is his other daughter and that she's still alive. She and Missy played their deception to the hilt. Fooled all of us." ·

Rebar swung his feet up onto an adjacent desk and leaned back in his chair. "Well, that's about to change. Tracking shows they've been busy girls today and it's still early. I figure they're gathering supplies for their next jaunt." He pointed to the main map on his monitor. "See all those purple blips? Shows every stop they made."

"We better hit the sack early tonight," Chamber added. "But first, I gotta make a call. See the two of you later."

CHAPTER TWO

Rebar untangled himself from his lovely lady, who had slept soundly in his arms all night. They'd enjoyed a quiet day yesterday, lazing about, watching purple blips move on the monitor then watching movies with Chamber until heading off to bed.

He dressed and quietly slipped downstairs to check the monitor—all looked quiet at dawn in Santa Fe, New Mexico. The sound of motorcycles disturbed the quietness of dawn. He wondered what a troop of bikers would be doing way out here, but then decided to look for Chamber.

Before he had a chance to find him, rapping sounded on his front door. After a quick glance out the window he furrowed his brows curiously when he saw several badass Harleys parked in his driveway. Bikers banging on his door? Maybe they were lost. He opened the door to four men and looked them over curiously. "Can I help you?"

"Hey, mate. Chamber about?" one of the men asked in a slight Texas drawl.

Chamber came out from the hall where he'd spent the night in one of the guest rooms. "Ah, good timing, mates. You got the message."

"This is the call you had to make?" Rebar couldn't withhold a grin.

"I wasn't about to let you and Halo trek to who knows where again without backup. Since Shade has intimidated the others, I called on my buddies from Ricochet."

"Welcome to my humble abode," Rebar told them with

14

light sarcasm.

"Nice cabin," one of the guys said as he gawked around.

"Lodge. It's a lodge." Rebar corrected. He always had to clarify that fact to visitors. He didn't live in a cabin. His home was elaborate and in no way resembled a cabin.

Chamber gave him a friendly slap on the back. "Relax, man." He chuckled. "Let's get introduced." He gestured toward the four men, all with dark hair dressed in jeans, boots and t-shirts. "Left to right, Rush, Shook, Levi, and Mossberg."

Rebar looked them over then arched one brow curiously. "Mossberg?"

"I'm a weapons specialist," the man said. "My friends call me Moss."

"I take it that's a nickname?"

Moss laughed. "I guess. Been going by that name so long it feels like I was born with it."

Rebar knew enough not to ask his birthname. When a man chose a code name or any other name to go by, his friends didn't disrespect the choice.

They all exchanged handshakes and cordial greetings.

"Where's everyone from?" asked Rebar. "Tell me about this club, Ricochet."

Before anyone replied, all heads turned toward the staircase leading to the upper loft. Cameo came trotting down the steps, wearing leggings and one of his shirts. She looked exquisite as always, no matter what she wore.

"Hey, sugar." He beckoned her over with an outstretched hand. "We have company." He introduced her to their new guests.

"Nice to meet you," she said in her sweet voice.

They looked her over as she did the same to them. Everyone stood there a few minutes, seemingly getting acquainted.

"Chamber called in reinforcements," he told her.

"I see." Her gaze swept over the bunch again. "Now there

are six of us."

"Make that eight," came a voice from the still-open door. Talon and Kohl strode inside, then closed the door.

Rebar couldn't hide his surprise. "You left Shade and Jackson?"

"We did," Talon replied without hesitation. "Chamber called last night and said it was time to choose. We've had your back since the day we met. Not bailing on you now."

"Besides," Kohl chimed in, "We know who the brain of the troop is. We'd rather run with the smart pack."

"Thanks." Rebar smiled gratefully. "I appreciate your loyalty and your friendship." He was surprised they chose him over Shade. Rarely had anyone done so.

"So, you wanna know about Ricochet?" Levi spoke up. Of the four, he was the only one with light-colored eyes. It was impossible not to notice the vivid blue in contrast to his midnight-black hair.

Rebar nodded. "Let's hang out in the main room. Anyone hungry or thirsty?"

"Nah, we're good," Moss replied. "We stopped at the café in town for breakfast. Good grub."

"Gabby's?"

"Yeah. How'd you know?"

"Only decent eatery that's open this early around here. Hey, make yourselves comfortable while Cameo and I grab a bite to eat."

"Who are those men?" Cameo asked as they downed a quick breakfast of scones and juice.

"Friends of Chamber's, I guess. Let's give them a chance."

"Okay." She followed him into the main room.

Rebar plopped into his favorite overstuffed leather chair and pulled Cameo onto his lap. "Before we get started, I just wanna say thanks in advance for your help. We have no idea what we're getting into."

Moss gave a nod, as did the others, indicating their acknowledgment of his appreciation. Once everyone was seated and settled, Levi resumed speaking.

"We formed Ricochet about twenty years ago. It started as a group of bikers helping homeless vets. We've evolved into a force of over fifty riders who rescue abused women and children in addition to continuing our work with veterans in need," Levi told him.

"We ride in small chapters to remain discreet. Makes it easier to get the women to safety without being tailed," Rush added. "The four of us always ride together. Our call of duty is primarily rescuing women."

Shook finally joined the conversation. "Getting women out of abusive situations and keeping them out is the most difficult task. Children are easier because we can get them to select fosters. Helping vets is tough at times because some have serious issues and don't wanna enter the shelters. But the women, they are so fragile coming out of abuse that it's hard to make them feel safe enough not to want to run back."

"Is that why you agreed to help find my mother?" Cameo asked. "Because you think she's being abused?"

Shook smiled adoringly at Cameo, which made Rebar remind himself to control any jealousy he might feel. After all, she was a rare jewel, extremely charismatic and no doubt the men found her alluring.

"From what Chamber told us, I'd say so. Hope you don't mind that he confided in us, the details of your dilemma."

"No. Not if you're here to help. And I trust Chamber. He's Rebar's best friend," she replied.

"That's a good thing," Shook replied with a smile. "We're not wasting our time then."

"Looks like we have a new force of eight." She glanced at Rebar and wondered how he'd met Chamber but didn't want to seem intrusive by asking. "Are you okay with this? I mean . . . it must hurt that four of your former comrades bailed."

Rebar shrugged casually. "I'm not surprised by Ammo and Bullet. They're followers not leaders. Yeah, I'm disappointed that Shade has taken such a hard stance. But we have what we need."

"So, what's the plan?" Shook asked. "Any idea where the woman's being held captive?"

"Not yet," Rebar replied. "I'm monitoring the activity of the General's daughters. Once they make their move, we'll make ours."

"How are you able to monitor them?"

"Through a tracking device."

Chamber laid a hand on Rebar's shoulder. "He's a genius. I told you guys about Eye Candy. He's come up with something even more advanced but not ready to go public with it. You're gonna have to trust me on this."

"We do," said Rush. "You've never given us reason not to."

Rebar observed the camaraderie between Chamber and these new guys. Obviously, they'd known each other quite a while and he began to wonder if Chamber had actually been riding with a different group all this time while pulling away from Shade. He wondered why his friend wouldn't have told him.

"I gotta get dressed." Rebar eased Cameo off his lap before pushing off the chair. "Make yourselves at home."

Cameo followed him upstairs. "What's wrong, baby?"

"Nothing really. Just wondering why Chamber never told me about this Ricochet group. He seems pretty tight with them."

"I didn't want to create conflict for you with Shade's troop," Chamber said from the doorway to the bedroom. "Can I come in?"

"You're already this far." Rebar laughed a little. "May as

well."

"So this is what the loft looks like completely finished and decorated." Chamber looked around. "Very nice and private."

"Not private anymore," Rebar scoffed. "How long have you been running with those guys?"

"Since the beginning. Sorry I never told you, but your connection to Shade . . . well, made things touchy. I didn't want the General to find out about Ricochet."

"Now that I've left the General's troop, you feel safe inviting your secret weapon in to help?"

Chamber half nodded half shrugged. "Something like that. I didn't want to put you in a tight spot. Are you pissed?"

Rebar pondered this while pulling on a shirt then socks. "No. I get it. The nature of Ricochet's mission requires utmost secrecy. Are they mercenaries?"

"No. nothing like that. We never charge for our help. Most of us have a loved one that's been down and out. That's what bound us together in the first place, our compassion for those in similar situations."

"I didn't know you had a family member caught in an abusive situation."

Chamber approached and stared him straight in the eye. "You, man. You're the one I've worried over all these years. Have you forgotten I was there when you first got out? We may not be related by blood, but I've always thought of you as my brother."

Rebar felt a surge of emotion. He stared down at the floor. "I haven't forgotten." Then he glanced at Cameo. "She doesn't know yet."

"Oh . . . sorry."

"Maybe it's time I told her, huh?" Rebar saw the questioning look sweep across her face. "All those times I thought you were out of the country you were running with these other guys?" He looked back at his friend.

"Mostly, yeah. I did spend a good bit of time down under to keep my cover."

Rebar did a quick mental recap of his friend's past and realized that Chamber had always been a rolling stone, drifting from place to place and nobody ever really knew when or where he'd show up, except for missions. The only place he'd crashed at most often was here, at the lodge.

"Ya know, you're one hell of a good secret keeper. Even I never suspected you worked with anyone else but the troop. You never missed an assignment."

"I never intended to keep you in the dark. But I always kept tabs on you, buddy. Once you made your break from the General, thanks to this lovely lady here, I knew it was only a matter of time before I got you into Ricochet," Chamber told him. "But the choice had to be yours. I didn't want to influence your decision. You needed to find out for yourself that the General is an evil prick."

Rebar's eyes widened. "You knew? Why'd you keep working for him?"

"To watch your back. We were the B-Team. No way would I leave while you were still there."

"That's why you're a drifter." He shook his head in amazement. "How'd you know about the General?"

"We've pulled victims out of a human trafficking ring that fingered him as the kingpin. But nobody's been able to get close enough to nab him." Chamber looked at Cameo. "Until now. She's the only person we know who's actually seen the man."

"Human trafficking? Damn. We've been working for a pervert all this time?" Rebar pulled Cameo to his side. "I'm so sorry you have to hear this."

"I'm okay. Everything lines up with what my mother told me about him. Finally, someone else knows the truth." She sounded almost relieved, but tension edged her voice. "Seems Ricochet has an agenda that reaches further than helping my mother."

"No agenda," Chamber refuted. "You asked for help. I found some. Better us, pretty lady, than a group of men loyal to that prick. If we get to take out a man on our wanted list at the same time, there's no shame. I'd never have asked you to put yourself in harm's way to help us nail him. Everything just kinda fell together. Maybe fate has finally decided to deliver some long overdue karma."

Her expression softened as did her voice. "I'm sorry. I didn't mean to insult your group. I'm very grateful for your kindness and your help. You were the only one who showed a hint of compassion when I first met the troop down at Shade's."

Chamber took her hand and gave it a gentle squeeze. "No worries, darlin. I understand your emotions are high right now. We all do."

"Thank you." Tears glistened in her lovely blue eyes.

"This is mind-blowing," Rebar said with a heavy sigh. "But I do believe karma is playing a role. What were the chances that I'd hook up with Cameo just as all this was coming to a head? And now I find out that my best friend belongs to a vigilante group that's after the man she fears most."

"I gotta admit the guys were all shocked when I told them about Cameo's plea for help." Chamber's eyes filled with mixed emotion. "I promise you that Ricochet won't give up until Malika is safe."

Cameo sniffed back tears and dabbed the corners of her eyes. "I'm overwhelmed by your kindness. I've hid from that beast all my life. I long for the day to break the invisible chains he's bound me with."

"Your day of release is on the horizon," Chamber said. "And the General's reign of terror is about to end."

Rebar took her into his arms for a hug. She trembled against him. He longed to take away her fear, ease her pain and erase the scars of evil that man had plagued her with way too long. She wrapped her arms around him and held tight. He kissed the top of her head.

"Soon, babydoll, soon. Justice will be served," he murmured near her ear.

She nodded but didn't say anything. He struggled with his feelings toward the four men who chose to remain loyal to the General instead of believing this tenderhearted woman and coming to her aid. He wondered how he'd ever feel close to Shade again. Brother or not—Shade let him down, while Chamber did the opposite. Chamber was more of a brother to him than Shade could ever be at this point.

While caught in that delicate moment, with Chamber quietly standing by, a loud screeching sound filled the house.

"What's that?" Her head jerked up suddenly.

"They're on the move," Rebar replied. "How long does Ricochet need to prepare?" he asked Chamber.

"Are you kidding?" Chamber cocked one brow. "These guys are ready to roll at a moment's notice. It's what we do. Why we don't put down roots."

"Let's go then." Rebar grabbed Cameo's hand and in a flash they were in his den. He whipped out his cellphone and synced it with the tracking modem. "Got it."

"You amaze me," Chamber said upon watching him in action.

He looked up with a slight grin. "Thanks."

"Time to roll, guys," Chamber announced as they hurried into the main room. He turned toward Rebar. "Any idea where they're headed?"

Rebar checked his device. "North. Strange. I thought surely he'd taken her south." He turned toward his girl. "You might want to do a quick change of clothes, look a bit more like

Camille to avoid suspicion."

"She's coming with us?" Shook asked, apprehension in his voice.

"We won't get close to him without her," Chamber told the men.

"I don't like taking a woman in," Rush said. "Too much can go wrong. We don't need her there."

"There's already a woman in there. I want to go," Cameo said then added with a huff, "And you might need me there. Don't be so cocky."

Rush blinked in surprise at her audacity but said no more on the matter.

"Believe me, she can hold her own," Rebar assured them. "I've seen her fight."

"We're all on bikes," Rush stated. "I assume you're going by car?"

"Yeah. My car is fast."

"I don't have a good feeling about taking her along but I'm not gonna waste time arguing over it. We've been after this guy for years." Rush looked her over. "She can come but she's waiting outside when we get there and you're gonna have to guard her. Once we know where the hostage is, we don't need your girl to get us through the door. This is a complicated mission."

"I won't get in the way," she said.

"All right," he reluctantly agreed. "But once your mother is out and on the way home, you're going with her while we go back and finish business. This is the closest we've gotten to him."

"Fair enough. Though I'd love to see him suffer, I'll do it your way," she consented. "I should change into more suitable street clothes anyway." She dashed upstairs.

Talon stepped forward. "Are we traveling or staying here to monitor tracking?"

Rebar thought for a moment. He hadn't even told them about his new tracking. Yet it would be beneficial to have someone watching homebase in the event he lost cell service as he had no clue yet as to the actual destination.

"I have a new system set up. It would be good to have someone I trust here to catch glitches if they pop up." He led them into the den and gave Talon and Kohl a crash course on the new readouts. "Easy, right?" he teased.

"No sweat," Kohl replied. "We've always been in sync with your technology."

"Awesome. Just watch those purple blips." He pointed to the screen. "Watch this bar, too. If the signal weakens, you'll have to call me and verbally relay the coordinates of those blips. Got it?"

"Got it." Talon pulled up a chair next to Kohl. "Don't worry, we've got your back. Now go do your thing."

Rebar gave them each a cordial pat on the back. "Thanks, guys."

They gave him a nod before he left to rejoin the others.

"Okay. Talon and Kohl are in place. I'm ready." He glanced toward the stairway to see Cameo on her way down, re-dressed in tattered jeans and a slinky half-top. From a distance he'd never know she wasn't Camille. Even closeup, if he didn't know her, he'd not tell them apart. He prayed the General wouldn't discover his ostracized daughter had returned from Europe.

"I'm riding with Rebar and his girl," Chamber told them. "We haven't spent time together in a long while."

The four members of Ricochet became silent for a minute or two, then Shook gave an approving nod. "It's good to see your friendship is still intact."

"Rebar is a welcome addition to Ricochet," added Rush. He seemed to grasp Chamber's subtle protectiveness over him. "He was smart to leave the General's troop on his own."

Moss and Levi nodded in accord. "We agree. Would do both of you good to catch up on the ride down to wherever we're headed," Levi said.

"I've missed my buddy, and I look forward to getting to know his lady. This is the first gal he's let this close to his heart. I would know." Chamber shot Rebar a knowing look and grinned. "Might be a good time to fill her in on a few things."

"Yes," Cameo agreed. "You were about to tell me something upstairs."

Rebar felt that familiar knot in his gut anytime the past came knocking but he couldn't, didn't want to hide it from Cameo forever. He felt Chamber was right. There would be no distractions while riding in his car to their destination. He trusted Cameo more than he'd ever trusted anyone before.

And if they were to continue leveling up their relationship, she'd need to know about the demons he'd conquered in the past—just in case they came calling again someday.

She'd been forthright with him regarding all her struggles and intimate details on extremely difficult subject matters, especially telling him about Malika. He owed her the same transparency to deepen their mutual trust.

"Yeah," he said softly, then dropped a quick kiss on her sweet lips. "I was and I will . . . once we get on the road."

Only one person knew what happened to him. He said a quick silent prayer that he wouldn't scare her away, by once again reliving that hell.

CHAPTER THREE

Cameo settled in the passenger seat of Rebar's vehicle for the lengthy road trip, wondering what secret Rebar had been afraid to confide in her. She'd been dangerously open with him about her life. She couldn't imagine he had anything scarier to reveal than what she herself had already endured.

"Whatever you need to tell me won't scare me away," she told him as they cruised onto the Interstate, heading south.

"I'm not a very social person," he admitted, casting her a nervous glance.

"I believe you already told me that." She reached over and grasping his free hand laced her fingers with his. "Just tell me about yourself. I won't run away. We've come too far. You're not getting rid of me that easy," she teased.

A warm smile touched his lips. "I'd never try to get rid of you, babydoll."

"Then what deep dark secrets haunt you that you've been afraid to let me in on?"

"I had a girl once. Long ago before I joined the military. I was a different man when I got out. PTSD hit hard. I'd seen so many comrades hooked on opioids, no way did I want to go down that road. I chose to deal with my mental and physical battle straight up, no chaser, no therapists, no groups."

"I admire your courage." She watched his face as he drove, trying to read his expressions.

"Well . . . my girl couldn't take it. She bailed on me one night after I had an episode. Didn't take her long to move on either. I suspect she had a man waiting in the wings. But I never bothered to find out for sure."

"I'm so sorry." Cameo felt sadness for him. Such an incredible man. She didn't understand how any woman could ditch this rare diamond of a guy.

"That's when I built the loft," he said. "She'd been living at my home while I worked down on the rigs with Shade. I trusted her. But when she announced her decision to cut bait and leave, I began to wonder if she'd had other men in my house. I withdrew from everyone except the troop. And even then, I only joined them for jobs, not social events. Chamber stayed with me frequently. Not sure I'd have stayed sober if not for him. I turned my bedroom into a guest room and added the third floor. Chamber helped me with most of the construction of it. Some days . . . we simply worked without saying a word."

"You poured your pain into work instead of a bottle. I'm impressed but not surprised. I've sensed a level of integrity in you that I've not seen in any other man."

He flashed a grateful smile then refocused on the road. "You're different. That's what I adore about you. No whining. No bitchy attitude. You're the coolest lady I've ever met. You have an independent spirit that I find irresistible. But you should know, some days, the PTSD sneaks up on me and those days can get quite dark."

"I remember what you said our first day in the loft. I'm honored that you trusted me enough to let me into that precious private world you labored over. Not only do I love that you built it yourself, but it has more meaning now than ever. You poured your blood, sweat and pain into that haven and chose me to share it with. There are no words to express how much that means to me." She leaned over and kissed the corner of his mouth. "I love you, baby. I don't care how dark it gets, I'll follow you down to the eye of the storm and hold you until it passes."

"Wow . . ." Chamber murmured from the back seat.

Cameo smiled slightly while studying Rebar's face. She couldn't see much from the side, but she could tell his emotions were swarming by the light twitch at the corner of his eye. He kept his gaze straight ahead, clutching the wheel with one hand and squeezing hers with the other. He let out a shaky sigh then glanced out his window for a split second.

"Yeah," he finally said, his voice cracking just a bit. "Wow . . ."

"I do believe you've found your soulmate," Chamber said in a quiet voice.

Rebar gave a quick nod and glanced over at Cameo. His eyes glistened with emotion. She offered him a reassuring smile.

"Is that what you're afraid of, my love?" she asked in a gentle nonintrusive tone. "That I'll bolt on your dark days? Or that if I found out another woman had lived in the lodge that I'd get jealous and leave?"

"Yeah." His voice remained soft and laden with feeling.

"Well . . . you just put that thought out of your head. Trust doesn't come easily to me, especially when it comes to men. But you've earned mine. And that's not an easy task as you know."

"I know, love." He lifted her hand to his lips and kissed her fingertips. "Thank you for giving me yours. I won't give you reason to regret it."

She glanced at the pack of impressive motorcycles in her sideview mirror. Chamber's secret pack of friends were riding their tail. Never could she ever have imagined that her life back in America would be like this.

When her mother convinced her to return home, Cameo had entertained visions of touring all the iconic sites like New York, California, the Grand Canyon and more. She figured Malika would take her to operas, theaters, and famous eateries — all the exciting places she'd heard of that were in the States.

It never entered her mind that she'd end up running into a twin she never knew existed, a troop of men that worked for the man she hated most, and now riding with an elusive club of bikers on a rescue mission.

"Can I ask you something?" She shifted her focus back to him.

"Anything, doll."

"Were you engaged to that girl?"

"Why does it matter? Living together, engaged . . . it's all commitment, right?"

"I guess. Just curious."

"Are you one of those women who need a ring on their finger as proof of my love?" he asked straight out, taking her off guard. "Will you be upset if I say, yeah, she was wearing my ring?"

"N-no . . ." She frowned and looked away, thwarted by his abrupt response. "I was just trying to get a feel for how deep your connection to her was. I may not be the jealous type but I'm still a real woman even if I do love muscle cars."

Chamber swatted Rebar upside the head. "Stop being an ass, man."

Rebar shrugged him off. "Sorry. Touchy subject."

"So you were engaged," Cameo pressed.

"Yeah. I thought I told you that I was engaged once and that it didn't work out." He let out a heavy sigh.

"Yes, you did but I wasn't sure if the one you're talking about was the one. I'm sorry."

"No . . . I'm sorry for snapping at you. Chamber's right. I was being an ass."

"You were hurt. I get it," she said softly, not wanting to agitate him further.

Rebar continued. "She had a big expensive rock on her

finger that she took with her when she left. Not that I care about the money. But damn, that was cold. I was in a bad place and she up and left, just like that. Didn't even have enough class to give me back the ring."

"I don't need a ring. Looking at all the divorces nowadays, a ring doesn't cement love or a relationship. I'm not even sure I want to get married. It's not something I've seen much of. No happy marriages in my family tree. None in yours either. Camille's wearing Shade's ring, but it doesn't stop her from flirting with you. So no, Rebar, I don't need a ring as proof. I just would rather you never compare me to that girl who burnt you. I'm not like most women."

"So you've said." He shot her a quirky look. "Again, I apologize for my crass remark. You're right, you're definitely unlike most women, for which I am grateful."

"I'm glad we got that settled. Seems we both have trust issues."

"We'll have to work on that," he said.

"I think we are. We're heading into a dangerous situation where trust is all we have, and a pack of rough riders on our tail."

"How's the tracking device going?" Chamber asked.

Rebar glanced at the phone propped on the console. "Still transmitting a strong signal. They're close to Raton, which puzzles me. There's not much in Raton except campgrounds."

"Doesn't sound much like villa territory," Cameo added. "Wonder what that man is up to. Joan did say he was taking her away for some privacy. Maybe he's taking her somewhere we'd never expect to look. He knows my mom isn't accustomed to outdoor living. She's used to city living and fine dining."

"That's right," Chamber said. "She was an actress, wasn't she?"

"Yes. I think she felt safe surrounded by people so that man couldn't hurt her. I guess she may have used it as a cover for her other affiliations, too, though."

"You know about her involvement with terrorists?" Chamber sounded surprised.

"She mentioned having unsavory contacts. I believe she was only using those to stay out of the General's reach. And maybe to aid in her plan to make him pay."

"Gutsy woman," Chamber remarked. "And perhaps a bit dangerous."

Cameo's eyes met his in the rearview mirror. "Desperate women do desperate things." When Rebar took his eyes off the road and glanced at her briefly, she gave him a scrutinizing look. "I sense there's more to your past you'd like to share. I get that the breakup hurt but you don't strike me as the type of man who'd let a woman bring you that low. What really happened that gave you PTSD? You never told me what causes the dark episodes. Do you trust me enough to tell me everything?"

"You're a thinker," he replied with a light laugh.

"Well?" She raised her brows expectantly.

"Yeah. I trust you." He looked at her again with a slight smile, yet apprehension shadowed his face. "We've got at least another hour on the road. Sure you can handle the ugly truth of war?"

"Baby, I endured my own horrendous war. Not that I'll revel in hearing yours. But I need to know what sets off your demons if I'm to be of any help when they come calling."

Rebar drew a deep breath then exhaled. His fingers tightened around the steering wheel. "My unit was closing in on a stronghold when we got pinned down. Everything happened so fast. Before backup arrived most of the troop had been brutally slaughtered. We took cover behind a tank, but the bastards threw a bomb under it . . ." He paused, his voice remained low and strangely composed, almost robotic. "Me and two buddies crawled to a ditch and shot as many of those rebel pricks as we could. We lost track of time while hunkered down and fighting for our lives."

Cameo whisked tears from her cheeks but remained silent.

After another brief pause, Rebar continued. "The Third Marine Raider Battalion arrived in time to save us. They obliterated those dirty Haji terrorists quickly. The three of us who survived in that ditch were flown to a field hospital. Spent a few weeks there before going back into the field."

"You had to go back into the war after all that?"

He gave a short nod. "Marines don't quit unless they're dead. We were given medals of valor for holding our ground until relief arrived. Over a dozen comrades died in that fight. The images of seeing my guys blown to pieces still haunt me."

"I'm very sorry." She squeezed his hand affectionately.

"Thanks. The carnage we saw that day . . . well, I don't need to go into detail. I'm sure you can imagine."

"Yes I can. But if you ever need to talk about it. I'm not fragile."

He gave her a grateful look. "I know."

"Keep your eyes on the road, hon," she admonished gently. "Did you stay in touch with the two other men who fought with you?"

"Once in a while we get together with the entire squad . . . what's left of them. It was a scene I try to forget but probably never will. My head was a mess when I received my discharge. I withdrew from society. Drifted from town to town until Chamber found me. We formed an instant bond. I told him about my family situation and that I had a brother in the States. He helped me get back on my feet, and hooked me up with Shade's crew."

Cameo glanced back at Chamber. "You're one of the good guys, aren't ya?"

He returned a warm smile. "I try. I've traveled around

Europe and Australia most of my life, in addition to America. Joined forces with Ricochet along the way. When I found Rebar, I couldn't leave him to his own. The mission of Ricochet is to help as many of those we can find that fall through the cracks of society."

"Yet you never told him about your affiliation with Shade and them," she noted curiously.

"I couldn't. His brother was already hooked tight into the General's network. I kept an eye on him, though, never lost touch."

"He's right," Rebar said. "No matter where Chamber was roaming about, I had his cell number and if I called, he came as quickly as he could. He's been my best mate since . . . geez, forever it seems."

"How did Chamber find you?"

Rebar kind of scoffed with a sardonic laugh. "Under a bridge. Like I told you before, my mom went to Heaven before I got out. I had nobody to go home to. She didn't own anything much and her flat was cleaned out by the time I made it back to Greece. I lived on my military pay. Took odd jobs."

"You didn't have a home?"

He shook his head. "Didn't know where to go. My head was a mess. Flashbacks and all that. Hated feeling confined. Didn't want Shade to see me as weak."

"That must've been horrible."

"Yeah, it wasn't pretty. Chamber talked me into staying with him. He had a small flat down in South Wales. It was peaceful. We talked often. He's a good listener. He just let me move at my own pace through the process of healing. When I felt stable enough, we returned to the States, and he got me a job on Shade's drilling rigs. I never wanted any of my father's estate as I never knew him. Shade insisted I accept my share. He knew Dad would've wanted it that way. So I used the money to build my lodge and start my inventions. I got my degree as a technical engineer in the Marines and now I'm putting it to use."

"I don't mean this to sound condescending, but I'm really proud of you. One, for serving your country so selflessly. And two, for fighting your way back without drugs, alcohol, or outside help." She studied his face for any signs of disapproval.

"You didn't offend me. I'm proud of me, too," he said with a light laugh then gave her a wink.

"So, you left Greece to go to the States to meet your brother and then you joined the Military here?"

"Yeah. My dad served. Shade was already in. I figured it was the honorable thing to do."

"Very honorable. You continue to impress me. Not only are you brilliant, but you're a skilled combat soldier and probably a decorated war hero."

His expression relaxed. She could tell her kind words pleased him. She waited for him to say more on the subject, but he didn't so she didn't either.

A few minutes later, Rebar looked at her again. "Now you know just about everything about me. Got your running shoes ready?"

"Never," she retorted with a scowl. "I value loyalty and honesty more than anything. Not to mention you're downright gorgeous. I'm not going anywhere, Rebar. And keep your eyes on that damn road."

"Neither am I, sugar. Neither am I."

Chamber pointed to the device. "Your purple blips have stopped moving."

Rebar stuck his hand out the window and motioned for the riders to pull over. They gathered at the next rest stop. He slid out from behind the wheel, tracking device in hand.

"We've got a destination point," he told the members of

Ricochet. "A campground in Raton. Willow Springs RV Park. Anyone here familiar with the area?"

Rush stepped forward. "Yep. The park will be filling up with bikers for the Run to Raton Rally. Takes place every July in Raton Pass."

"I can't believe it's July already," Cameo muttered, realizing her fortieth birthday was coming up in a couple days.

"Didn't you say you were born on the fourth of July?" Rebar asked.

"Yeah. No big deal. Forty isn't exactly an age every woman looks forward to." She laughed.

"You're turning forty?" Rush lifted his brows.

"Sshh," she hushed.

"Damn, woman. You look good. I thought you were just around thirty," he countered.

Rebar raised a brow at Rush's comment but held his tongue.

"You're very kind." She smiled, touched by his unnecessary flattery. "Youthful looks run on my maternal side. Wait till you see my mother. She's almost sixty, and stunning."

"I have no doubt. Sorry you gotta spend your special day doing this."

"No worries. I'm far from spoiled, and I don't have a princess complex."

She noticed Rush studying her for a few moments. He stood tall, like Rebar and Chamber. His long wavy black hair framed a ruggedly handsome face. She couldn't see his eyes through the dark sunglasses but imagined they were dark, too. She liked that he seemed friendlier toward her now.

"Does Ricochet have a leader?" she asked.

"You're looking at him, sweetheart," he replied, pride in his voice. He slid his shades to the top of his head to look at Rebar's tracking device. "Let us know if they move. We're less than twenty minutes away from that campground."

"Wonder why he took her there," Cameo dipped puzzled brows.

"To blend," Rush told her. "If he's in an RV in a place swarming with other campers and bikers, it'll be harder for us to find him."

"Not with this," Rebar interjected. "We'll find Joan or Missy and follow them. None of them suspect we have the capability to track. And they'll never expect bikers to be looking for them."

"Good point." Rush gave Rebar a cordial shoulder squeeze as men did sometimes. "Good work."

"Remember, nobody is to use Cameo's name if we end up face-to-face with them. She's *Halo*. The General doesn't know the daughter he sent away decades ago has returned. If he suspects it's her, things could get crazier than they already are," Rebar reminded them. "Halo was Camille's code name during the Malika takedown. The old man thinks that only Camille and his troop know that name."

Ricochet members nodded in accord.

"Got it." Rush gave Cameo one more dissecting look before placing his shades back over his eyes.

She stared back at him, after having had a good glimpse of his face for the first time, especially those eyes. He had the same shadowy midnight eyes as Rebar and Shade. She was intrigued over the uncanny resemblance he bore to Rebar. If she didn't know better, she'd think Tassos had fathered another son that nobody knew about. After all, Rebar's history was a closet of never-ending secrets that continued to be unveiled.

"There's a service station with a red roof right before the entrance to the campground," Rush told them. "You can't miss it. A big yellow sign with *Welcome to Raton* on it. Stop there. I know the owner. I'll ask him to pull your car into his garage to keep it safe."

"You want me to leave my car in the hands of a stranger in New Mexico?" Rebar balked.

Rush chuckled. "You can't rumble into the campground in that." He gestured toward Rebar's gleaming black Gran Sport. "You may as well wave red flags and shout, we're here! Malika will be gone in a flash."

Rebar turned toward Cameo. She cringed apologetically with a sheepish smile.

"I'm sorry . . . I know how you feel. But we decided to trust these guys. I'm sure Rush knows what he's doing."

Rush turned toward Rebar again. "You ride bitch with Chamber, he can take Levi's bike. Levi will double up with Moss since we're short on bikes. Actually that's a good thing. We need to blend if we're to follow his daughters back to wherever he's holding the woman. Four bikes are less conspicuous than eight. Shook needs to ride solo since he's the one going inside for the hostage." Then he directed his attention back to Cameo once more. "*Halo* . . . ride on back with me. Tuck that lovely blonde hair under a helmet and keep your face at my back. Should Missy or Joan spot us before we find them, we don't want them recognizing you." He pulled a leather riding jacket from the saddlebag of his bike. "Put this on. We always carry extra to disguise women."

Cameo gave a nod of compliance. Rebar said nothing further. She felt bad about bringing this into his life. He'd had a hard enough time overcoming serious challenges. He didn't deserve to bear her burdens, too.

"I know what you're thinking," he said out of the blue. "You're worried this is too much for me after what I told you."

"Reading my mind again?" She smiled.

"I feel your thoughts. And don't worry, I can handle it. I'd rather be charging down the enemy than sitting around as an idle target for demons." He placed a sweet kiss on her lips.

"Like I said, if I don't keep my brain busy, it leaves me open for sneak attacks from the past. Let's do this, girl."

CHAPTER FOUR

A huge golden sun dipped low in the sky as Ricochet rolled into Raton. Cameo did as instructed, and had stuffed her hair beneath a helmet, keeping her face discreetly against Rush's back. She had the pleasure of breathing in the scent of his black leather jacket and sensual cologne while sitting behind him on a magnificent Harley.

Just as Rush had said, the manager of the service station had pulled Rebar's cherished car into his garage and closed the door with the promise of keeping her safe until their return. Cameo was impressed with this motorcycle club's influence. She'd never ridden one before and found the experience exhilarating, especially when he picked up speed on open stretches.

Willow Springs Park was huge and packed with bikers and RVs. She wondered if they'd truly get lucky enough to pin down Joan or Missy's exact location using Face Palm. Everything regarding this mission was out of her hands.

Chamber had summoned a new troop of men, fierce, strong-looking men who seemed quite streetwise.

And Rush was leading the rescue.

All these amazing men going out of their way to help her, a woman they'd never met before today. Talon and Kohl had chosen Rebar over Shade and joined them, for which she was grateful. She'd not known chivalry like this—ever.

Their group of seven astride four impressive Harley's rumbled peacefully throughout the park. Shook was the only one riding without a passenger, so he fell back to watch their tails.

Rush led. Chamber and Rebar stayed tucked within the pack to remain discreet. Moss and Levi rode close behind them.

They hadn't gone very far before Rush pulled over into the lot of a small market. Baskets of produce sat in rows under the tin roof of a little shack. Streaks of late day sunlight sparkled off jars of homemade cider standing in a neat row on the dirt floor.

"What's wrong?" she asked him.

"I saw Chamber signal from my sideview mirror. Something must be up."

The four bikes growled to a halt.

Rebar slid off the back and approached. "They've stopped moving." He pointed to his tracking unit. "Do you know where this watering hole is? Seems they've gone out for drinks at a place called Margaritas."

"Yeah. It's about fifty feet that way." Rush pointed toward the sunset. "We're practically on top of them."

"Perfect. Take us to a spot where we can watch and wait."

"No problem." Rush fired up his engine.

Rebar dropped a quick kiss on Cameo's lips before hopping back on Chamber's bike. The four bikes cruised down a one lane dirt road that led deeper into the campground until they arrived at a rundown bar. Several surly-looking men sat on the ground along the left wall, sombreros pulled down low and bottles of beer in their hands. They barely looked up.

She assumed this little town was accustomed to bikers riding through from what Rush had said. Never did she picture, when pondering her future, that she'd be riding down to a dusty town just south of the Colorado border, on the back of a Harley, to rescue a mother she'd never seen until a month ago.

I must be crazy. She thought to herself. *Does my mother even want to be rescued?* Missy's words crept back into her head, but she shoved them aside. She refused to believe Malika, in all her class and beauty, would have any kind of twisted affair with that man. *I'm just fatigued from the heat and nervous because we're about to find them.*

Rush guided his Harley to the far side of the dirt parking area and parked under a scant grove of trees. She glanced up. There weren't more than three scrawny trees, and they didn't offer any shade. She was glad the sun had gone down to ease some of the day's heat.

Chamber parked beside them, then Moss and Levi beside him. Shook pulled his bike to the other side of Rush, placing her and Rebar in the middle of the pack. Shook cut the engine and leaned back on his seat with his boots propped on the handlebars and both arms folded behind his head. He appeared quite casual and rather sexy sprawled out across a silver and black Harley.

In fact, she hadn't seen a homely man among Rebar's friends on either side. The only one she found slightly less appealing was Ammo with his tattooed bald head. She wasn't a fan of that look. And his partner Bullet's cropped red hair didn't appeal to her either. Though she was refined, she found men with longer hair and rebel appearance most attractive.

Maybe it's an opposites attract thing, she inwardly mused. *Polished city girl drawn to renegade bikers.* She never considered herself overly sophisticated despite her strict upbringing by the mams because her career choice had taken her into extremely remote areas of jungles and wilderness. She wasn't afraid to get dirt under her nails. Yet she also never envisioned herself running with a pack of vigilantes either.

Regardless, here she was, doing just that.

A sudden movement to her left drew her from her thoughts. Rebar and Chamber had come to full alert and signaled to Rush that the two women who'd just exited the cantina were their targets.

Rush gave a nod then subtly got the attention of his pack. They casually resumed positions ready to ride.

Cameo watched Missy stagger sloppily beside Joan who nudged her playfully and tugged at her sister's pink-blonde hair. The two women made their way to a small white car, and after much giggling and horseplay they finally got in.

Great. Two drunks and one is driving. Cameo rolled her eyes in disgust. But their inebriated state fell to Ricochet's favor. They'd be able to tail the women with relative ease and not get noticed.

After Missy and Joan had merged onto the road, the pack started their engines and calmly followed from a distance. Rebar's new invention had worked great and would be priceless once he was ready to market Face Palm. She marveled over how one coincidental crazy meeting in a gas station parking lot had led her to the love of her life.

The boxy white car turned a corner then bumped along a windy gravel road past rows of campsites crowded with RVs and motorcycles. Rush had proven to be right again. They'd never have found the General in this mess if not for the tracking device. He and Rebar made a good team it seemed.

Eventually the white car up ahead slowed and pulled into a short drive then parked in front of a very luxurious RV. She'd seen some of the more deluxe models during her assignments to the outback. They were impressive with air conditioning, TVs, lush interiors and even Wi-Fi. She figured the General's camper would be fully loaded — in more ways than one.

Rush led the pack right past the campsite, glancing over as he did. Cameo assumed they were surveying the scene before devising their strategy. And most likely they'd make their move under the cover of night.

They gathered at an empty site on a cul-de-sac several lots down. "We'll make camp here," he told everyone after they'd parked and dismounted.

She took a look around. They were tightly nestled between

other biker groups camping in the same circle. *Good cover*, she thought, impressed by his leadership thus far.

"Hey, sugar," Rebar approached, lifted her hand to his lips and kissed her fingertips. "How ya holding up?

"Okay . . . I think." She shrugged. "Nervous."

"Sorry you had to ride with a stranger. I wasn't gonna argue with him. He seems like a good guy and knows what he's doing."

"It's okay. I didn't mind. I felt safe on the back of his bike. I agree with you. He does seem to have our safety at the top of his list."

"Guess they've been doing this a long time."

Chamber walked up to them. "Hey, you guys alright?"

"Yeah. Just talking." Rebar glanced at his phone when a signal light flashed. "Message from Talon. He said tracking on homeport is glitching out."

"Could it be wearing off?" Cameo wondered aloud.

"Possibly. It's been a few days since we slipped it on them. I haven't perfected it yet. They looked drunk at the bar. The liquor could've had an effect."

"Good thing we didn't waste time," she said.

"Very good thing," Rebar agreed, then looked at Chamber. "Tell Rush we've lost tracking."

Chamber gave a nod then walked away.

"This Ricochet gang fascinates me," she told Rebar. "I've never known any bikers. I always thought they were scary. But these guys are super cool."

Before they could continue their conversation, Rush and his pack strolled over to them.

"We'll move in a few hours after dark," Rush said. "Levi and Moss are riding down to watch their site. I don't want the two bitches slipping away now."

"Sorry about the tracking glitch. My device is still in the testing phase," Rebar told him.

"Hey, no need to apologize. Your invention got us this far. It's up to us now. We rarely lose a target once we find them. You did good, man."

A modest grateful expression traversed Rebar's face. "Thanks."

"Do you have a plan in place?" Cameo asked.

Rush nodded. "We'll break camp here and ride down. Moss and Levi will cover the back. The rest of us will guard the front while Shook goes in and grabs your mom. That way, we'll all be ready to ride once he has her on his bike."

"Do you think they're armed?"

"Baby, I've learned to expect anything." Rush dipped one brow with an air of confidence about him. "From what Chamber told me, the General's daughters are ruthless and unpredictable."

"Yeah . . . I guess so." She thought back to what Camille had told her about the bayou, then about her own recent encounter with the crazed sisters.

"We're prepared to go in and fight if Shook runs into more than he can handle. He's highly skilled in combat and recon. Shouldn't be hard to find your mother inside an RV. Might get confusing and messy if we all barged in."

"True. At least you don't have to roam through his mansion, like we did."

"The only trouble I worry about is if the captive freaks out when Shook goes in. I just hope your mother wants to be rescued and is smart enough to trust us right away."

Cameo let out a nervous sigh. "Me, too."

Chapter Five

Stars sprayed a vast southwestern sky on a new moon. Other than those tiny twinkling lights millions of miles away, the night was black as coal. She and Rebar had been lying on a blanket pulled from one of the guys' saddlebags. They made a little small talk but mostly dozed off and on while waiting for go-time.

Around midnight, Chamber sauntered over. "Hey," he said quietly. "Rush said it's time to ride."

Cameo tried to calm the knot in her gut as she folded the blanket and handed it back to Chamber. Rebar appeared calm as ever. Nothing seemed to rattle him.

Everyone mounted up and the bikes growled to life. Nobody revved the engines to avoid attention, especially from sleeping campers that would be aggravated by the noise of the bikes starting up as it was. They kept their presence as quiet as possible as they cruised a short distance down the gravel road to the General's lot.

Moss and Levi veered between two lots farther down then vanished from sight. She assumed they were doing as planned. Rush gestured toward Chamber who then parked alongside the road several feet away. None of the guys cut their engines but kept them on a low idle except for Shook. He parked his Harley between the General's RV and the one next to it.

Cameo watched anxiously as Shook slipped off his bike and crept stealthily toward the camper where Malika was held captive. He had tied his hair back and wore a black sleeveless tee, jeans, and boots. His appearance reminded her of a character she might see in a Rambo movie.

She waited in tense silence, frequently glancing at Chamber and Rebar for comfort. Rebar gave her a reassuring wink. His stoicism impressed her, yet she couldn't help but wonder what thoughts were running through his mind at this very moment, especially after what he'd shared with her on the ride down to Raton. She prayed this incident wouldn't trigger a flashback or set off his PTSD. She'd feel horrible if her drama brought him more distress.

The sound of muffled voices and scuffling snapped her from thought. Everyone's focus shifted toward the oversized camper. Not long after, Shook emerged from the RV with her mother. He pushed her along in front of him as they kept their heads lowered and zigzagged toward his bike. He hopped on and Malika didn't hesitate to jump on behind him. Within seconds, he was speeding down the berm of the gravel lane toward the main road.

Chamber and Rush followed. She didn't know much about riding motorcycles but assumed they were riding the berm to avoid skidding in the gravel. Chamber and Rebar fell in behind Shook as she and Rush tailed close behind.

The lane was long and seemed difficult to navigate for the large motorcycles by the way Rush was driving. He seemed to be taking extra caution to avoid the gravel during their escape. And with each man carrying a passenger now, the drivers probably needed to use extra caution on the uneven terrain.

Cameo barely took a breath as they made their way down. Her nerves were on edge. After what felt like forever, but was actually merely minutes, they merged onto a paved road and hooked up with Moss and Levi who were waiting at the intersection. The four Harleys picked up speed.

She saw the gas station sheltering Rebar's car come into

view. Shook turned into the parking lot. They'd need to move fast to get Rebar's car and back on the road. She knew the General wouldn't let Malika go that easily. Chamber swung into the lot a few minutes behind Shook. Just as Rush geared down to follow, a sequence of loud pops then a hiss filled the air.

Everything from that point felt like slow motion. Cameo felt the bike going down but was powerless except to cling to Rush's waist as they hit the pavement. Pain and fear engulfed her. He'd lost control. Had he been hit? She wasn't even sure he was conscious.

Sudden chaos ensued. She heard rapid gunfire. Shuffling footsteps. Muddled voices. Then the unmistakable sound of racking the slide of a gun followed by the crack of a whip—a sound she'd never forget. Something she'd never told Rebar was just how the General, her supposed father, had terrorized her.

"Get up," a gruff voice bellowed.

She struggled to clear her head while looking up. A monster stood over her, dressed in full military fatigues, his bearded face twisted into a scowl. As her vision cleared, she glared back into the steely gray eyes of the man she hated more than anything.

What happened to Ricochet? The thought sliced through her confusion. She tried to look around, but the sting of a leather strap forced her into a curled ball, both arms crossed over her face.

"Your friends have been subdued," he snarled. "If you want them to live, get on your feet. You and this piece of rebel scum."

"My mother . . ." she muttered.

"She's gone," he stated coldly. "So much for loyalty among comrades, eh *Halo*?" he sneered with a deliberate taunt. "One of your men took off with her. The rest are down and out. But

I'll settle for you, my dear, and this joke of a man. The two of you will make excellent bargaining chips. Did you really think you could get away with taking Malika?" His evil laugh made her cringe.

"Go to Hell," she seethed through clenched teeth.

"Let's go," he barked. "Or Missy will put a final bullet into your friends."

She heard Rush moan beside her. Glancing over, she was horrorstricken to see a pool of blood under him. In her foggy state of mind, she recognized Joan. The butch woman hoisted Rush's body up and dragged him away.

"Where's she taking him?"

The whip snapped across her bare arm. She recoiled in pain. Tears filled her eyes.

"To my vehicle. Now get moving if you want your precious Rebar to live."

Pushing through the pain, Cameo got to her feet. The General shoved her along behind Joan and Rush. An uncanny flashback washed through her as some of Camille's story felt suddenly familiar. As she struggled along, she saw four bodies writhing on the street — Moss, Levi, Chamber and Rebar!

Oh no! Tears felt like streaks of fire streaming down her cheeks. *No, no, no. I've done this to him. Camille was right to stay away. All these men, hurt because of me.* She could barely stand the agony of it all. *But her mother was safe. Was it worth it?* She wondered silently.

There wasn't a soul around in the dark of night as the General forced her and Rush into a Hummer. They hadn't seen this vehicle in the lot. He must've had it hidden. She wasn't surprised a man like him would have backup plans. He was as evil as they came.

Now would be a good time for my sister the nurse to show up. She winced at the thought. These people assumed she'd know how to care of Rush. They thought she was Camille, a registered nurse. They couldn't be more wrong. She knew how to tend animals but had never done first-aid on a human.

After she and Rush were locked into the Hummer, Cameo peered out a tiny window and saw Missy leaving the rest of Ricochet on the ground to fend for themselves. She trotted over to the vehicle and hopped into the front seat. Joan sat in the third-row seat behind them with a rifle in hand.

The vehicle began to move but not back toward the campsite. They were heading away as the gas station was on the opposite side of the road from when they rode in. Cameo worried over where the General was taking them. There'd be no way for Rebar to track anyone this time.

Rush began to stir beside her. "Where are we?" he barely whispered in a strained voice.

"Not in a good place," she replied quietly.

"What happened?" He placed a hand over his side. "I'm bleeding. This can't be good."

"We've been taken hostage."

"Where are the others?"

"Shook got away but the rest are lying on the road back at the station. I don't know how badly hurt they are. It all happened so fast."

Rush flopped his head back on the seat with a sigh. "Bloody hell. I don't know where I failed."

"They ambushed us from behind."

"Did anyone else survive?" he asked with a devasted expression.

"I'm not sure. I saw them moving just as we got thrown in the Hummer."

Missy twisted around from the front seat. "Your friends will live. I only used a stunner on them."

Cameo glared at the wench. "I heard a lot of gunfire and Rush obviously took a bullet."

"Yeah," she replied sharply. "The bullets were to stop you and Malika. Your comrades returned fire. Malika got away with one of your guys but at least we got you. She won't let her daughter take the fall. And those guys will probably want their buddy back."

Joan piped up from behind. "Why don't you do your nursey thing and help this man?"

"I don't have a first-aid kit. If he dies, you'll go down for murder."

"Nah. Daddy knows people. Besides, your new boyfriend here isn't gonna die," Joan retorted in her grating voice.

"Too much chatter back there!" The General snapped from behind the wheel. "No more talking until we get home."

Cameo slunk back against Rush and silently prayed for help. He closed his eyes and leaned against her, groaning softly. She racked her brain over how this happened and how they'd get out.

What would Malika do? I'm my mother's child. I'm not Camille. I gotta pull myself together and do something. Nobody knows who I am, and no one knows the General like I do.

She pulled Rush's jacket in around him to keep him warm though the weather was hot and dry. She didn't want him going into shock. She figured to tend him just like she'd tended all the wounded animals in the wilderness. She looked at the spreading stain on Rush's shirt and wriggled out of the biker jacket they'd given her, then rolled it up inside-out and eased it under his shirt. "Press on this," she told him softly and taking his hand placed it on the wad.

What was ahead? She had to be sure to continue playing her part ... to be Halo. This wasn't how she'd handle a wounded animal of course, but she'd read books and seen plenty of movies and hoped the pressure on the wound would help lessen the bleeding. If Rush remained conscious. If not, she'd have to take over. It was as first-aid as she could make it for now ... And if they told her to deal with the wound later, it wasn't as if she'd never removed a bullet from an unfortunate animal. A human wasn't that much different.

This family of psychos would not uncover her true identity if she could help it.

Dawn crested the horizon as the Hummer pulled up to a familiar mansion. To Cameo's surprise, their abductors had taken them back to the General's mansion in Santa Fe. After roughly ushering her and Rush along and into the house, the poor man stumbling, they forced them upstairs and into a guest suite where Joan shoved them into separate chairs.

Missy hung back near the doorway, observing with a scrutinizing stare. "You've certainly made a lot of new ... friends," she pointed out while casually toying with her weapon. "Shade never mentioned these guys. I wonder ... does he know who you've been running around with?"

Cameo sensed Missy picking up vibes and realized her stint as Camille may end sooner than expected. They needed to find a way out of this place and soon. There was no time to wait on the so-called mention of a bargain.

"Stay put if you want to live," Joan barked. "One sneaky move and the dude takes a final bullet and you come with me, fluffy."

"Go get the first-aid bag from my den," the General told his daughters. "Then prepare some food for our *guests*."

Missy and Joan disappeared.

"Now," he said upon flipping a chair around and straddling it to face them. "I want Malika back. She belongs to me, and you had no business taking her." He rubbed his chin and stared at her through narrowed eyes. "I am baffled, though, over how the hell you managed to find us. Malika had no phone and no way of contacting you. How'd you do it, Camille?"

Cameo scoffed. "I have my ways. You think you're all that. That group of men has more intelligence in their pack of eight than you had in your entire squadron."

"You've become quite a sassy wench. Doesn't Shade keep you in line, girl?"

"I don't need a man to keep me in line, old man."

He pushed off the chair and retrieved his leather crop. Shivers ran down her spine, but she refused to let him see her terror. She bit her lower lip to hide the trembling.

"You *will* tell me how your pathetic troop found us. Nobody knew our coordinates . . . not a soul."

"Well . . . *we* did, so chew on that a while, ya old coot."

He tilted his head suspiciously. *"Who* are you?"

She lifted her chin defiantly. "Secret Agent Halo, sir," she mocked.

He raised his arm and brought the crop down hard across her back. She cried out, then gritted her teeth.

"Tell me how you found me. Who's the leak in my troop? Do you want to pay for their treachery?"

"Nobody betrayed you. I'm the secret weapon."

"Bullshit! You're just a fragile little girl playing with the big boys. You're out of your league here. Now tell me which man in my regiment has betrayed me!"

"None of them."

The crop stung her back again. Tears welled in her eyes.

"You will tell me if I have to beat it out of you."

"Shade won't be happy to find out you've hurt his woman," she hissed.

"Shade is my most loyal soldier. I'm thinking maybe Rebar is the one. I was shocked to hear he came to the house with you. Maybe I should've put a bullet in *him* instead of *this* bastard. Who is this guy anyway?"

"A friend," she muttered.

"Since when do you have male friends outside the troop?" He glared at her in open skepticism. "You showed up at my house with Rebar, and now this guy. Has your mother finally worn off on you? Is Malika turning you into a whore, just like her?"

"You spineless prick. Not everyone bows to you. You picked the wrong battle, old man, when you chose to strike me." Anger rose in her soul, triggering flashbacks.

"You're much tougher than the men have let on. Let's see just how tough you really are." He reached out with one weathered hand and ripped her shirt up and over her head and tossed it on the floor. Then a stunned look crossed his ugly cratered face. "You're not Camille! You're the other one. When did you . . . how'd you . . ." he seemed at a loss for words.

"What's wrong?" she taunted, knowing he'd recognize the scars on her back. "Can't even remember your other daughter's name?"

"Malika found you?"

"I know everything. Every sordid detail of what you did to my mother forty years ago. I spent my entire life vowing you'd pay one day for what you did to me, but Mother beat me to it. Well . . . she tried."

His face went ashen as he staggered back in shock. "You're your mother's child alright. And you'll never tell a single soul what you know. Nor will your slut of a mother." He brought the crop down harder.

Rush shouted for him to stop. Even in his weakened state, he fought to stay conscious. "You'll pay for this!"

"Who will make me pay?" The General laughed sadistically. "You? Your little pack of biker friends we left lying on the road?" Then he turned back toward Cameo. "I demand to know how you found us!"

Cameo scowled at him. "Never."

His rage exploded. A string of profanity spewed from his mouth as he knocked her to the floor.

He whipped her relentlessly without mercy. She refused to cry out. Though tears burnt her cheeks and her body ached from his strikes, she held her tongue.

Her pride gave her courage and no matter what this bastard did, she'd never give up Rebar's secret tracking device. Thanks to it, they'd saved Malika from a horrid fate.

When he'd unleashed all his rage, he kicked her shirt on the floor beside her. "Get dressed, whore. I'm done for now."

He stomped out the door and slammed it shut. Cameo collapsed in a heap and burst into sobs. She managed to pull her shirt on despite the pain. Then she crawled to Rush and untied him.

"Sweet baby . . ." he muttered in a choked-up voice. "Dear God. How'd you survive that man?" He reached for her.

She didn't have an answer. "We need to get out of here. Can you walk at all? You've lost a lot of blood."

"Not the first time," he replied. "After what I just saw, I will run beside you, if that's what it takes."

Their eyes met in an intense exchange of desperation. He framed her face between gentle hands. "You are the bravest person I've ever known. Forgive me for this." He leaned over her and placed a tender kiss on her lips.

"Forgive you?" She blinked tears from her eyes.

"For kissing you."

"No apologies. Any comfort at this point is welcome. Let's get the hell outta here. Before he finishes what he started. He probably went to polish off a bottle and snooze. That's what he used to do when I was little."

"What about Missy and Joan? They're coming back with a first-aid kit."

Cameo pointed toward a far wall. "I can deal with those two bitches. Look at all that stuff. He loves his weapons. Hangs them in every room. Take your pick."

They leaned on each other while hobbling across the room. Cameo pulled a crossbow off the wall. "I hate him. He has a trophy room where all his kills are mounted to the wall. He's exactly the enemy I work against in the wild."

"You know how to use that thing?"

"Yep. I don't have time to explain."

He arched one brow then lifted a loaded assault rifle off a rack. "Not as quiet but we may need more power on the run."

"Can you help me load this thing? Under normal circumstances I could but I'm hurting," Cameo asked.

"Yeah." He winced with pain but together they got the arrows into place and cocked.

"There's a rear exit right down the hall if he hasn't sealed it off," she told him. "It leads to two flights of steps to the ground floor and into the back yard. We should make a break for that instead of the front door. I don't really think we're in shape for a fight."

"I agree." He no sooner spoke than footsteps sounded outside the room.

"Fluffy . . . oh, fluffy . . ." Joan called in a singsong voice. "I've got everything you need to fix up your biker boy. Missy's cooking up some grub. Remember how we did things at the cabin?" The door swung open and in walked Joan, smiling as if nothing were wrong. "Just like old times, huh, fluffy?" she cooed, closing the door behind her then looking up.

Whoosh! Whoosh! Whoosh! Cameo didn't hesitate to release the trigger.

Joan never made a sound as her body hit the door and hung there, her head flopped to her chest. All three arrows nailed their target spot-on.

"Damn, woman. You don't mess around." Rush shot her a hot look.

"That bitch isn't coming back to life this time. Not on my watch."

"I see that." He seemed a bit shocked.

"Let's go before Missy shows up." She glanced at Rush,

who stood frozen in place while staring at Joan's body hanging on the door, pinned by the arrows. "C'mon," she urged then dropped the crossbow.

They made their way down the hall and much to her relief, the rear exit was just as it was when she lived there as a child. A vivid recollection of racing down the stairs to escape that whip flashed before her. Cameo shook it off and kept moving. She and Rush crept quickly as possible to the ground floor and out the back door.

Cameo gulped in fresh air the moment they left the house. They tried to run but mostly limped their way out of sight. A high noon sun beat down on their wounded bodies. She knew the General would probably be passed out drunk by now. He'd always guzzled liquor before dropping off into a deep sleep for his daily siesta. And to wake him incurred serious punishment. She wasn't sure how long Missy would take to bring the food up.

"I hope the guys are okay," she murmured as they hurried along. "We need to reach a phone. I have no idea where my purse is. I apologize for not knowing the area. I only lived here till I was five. The only way I found his home address is from my boarding school records."

"You don't owe anyone an apology, girl. And I'll be the first to eat my words over not needing you here."

"Don't worry. I won't gloat." She smirked lightly.

He began to laugh but stopped and clutched his side, then dug in his pockets. "Seems they took my phone, too. And my wallet. We're on our own here, babe."

She looked up at him and mustered a hopeful smile. "But we're free."

CHAPTER SIX

"I'm not going back to Denver without her," Rebar stated as he and the rest of Ricochet sheltered in the Raton garage where his car had been parked.

"We need help, mate," Chamber argued. "Shook took off with Malika. It's just you, me, Moss, and Levi. And we're beat up pretty bad."

"She's out there somewhere, with Rush. They're probably injured. I'm not leaving without them." His gaze moved around the small group. "What the hell happened anyway?"

"I think they used stun guns on us," Moss said.

"I heard a lot of gunfire," Levi added.

"They must've been aiming for Shook to stop him from getting away with Malika." Chamber rubbed his chafed arms. "Damn, what a fall."

Rebar felt sore as well. All of them were scraped up from hitting the pavement but other than minor injuries, and some road burn, they'd come out of the chaos fairly unscathed compared to what could've been. "I think Rush took a bullet," he said. "While lying on the road writhing in pain, I saw him lying next to Cameo. He looked unconscious."

"I don't know how you managed to see anything," Chamber said. "That blonde kept hitting repeat on her stunner. My mind blacked out a few times."

"I didn't want to lose sight of Cameo. It's what kept me focused."

Chamber let out a sigh. "This is bad, man."

"Shook got away. He'll get Malika to safety and come back

for us. Maybe he'll bring reinforcements. Either way, we gotta try and find our friends. I should've given everyone Eye Candy. Dammit."

"Don't beat yourself up over it. Ricochet has gone up against a lot of tough situations but this one was unusual."

"Probably because they're terrorists," Rebar noted.

"Hey," Moss interjected. "We accomplished what we came down for. We got Cameo's mother out and away. There's always a risk of complications with any mission. If Rush survived, he'll take good care of your girl."

"He survived," Rebar said. "I can't think of it any other way. If I picture Cameo alone with that prick and his two crazed daughters, my mind goes to dark places. I've got my car. I'm going looking for them."

Chamber gave a relenting nod. "I won't let you go alone. I'm giving you back your bike, Levi. I'll ride with Rebar."

"We'll come with you," Levi said. "Ricochet doesn't rest until the run is done. And this ain't done till we bring our leader and your girl home."

"That's right," agreed Moss. "With two bikes and Rebar's car, we stand a better chance of finding them. I'm glad Shook got Cameo's mother away. One less body to worry about."

"Thanks, guys." Rebar looked from one to another, grateful for their stamina, courage, and camaraderie. "Are we ready to ride?"

"Yup." Moss pulled himself up. "As soon as the bikes are ready. The mechanic is going over them. Not sure Rush's bike can be saved. They hit the road hard."

"Rush has solid connections here." Rebar tried keeping his thoughts trained on a positive outcome.

Moss nodded. "We're well known in the biker world."

"And respected," Levi added.

Rebar gave him a nod. "You've earned my respect, that's for damn sure."

Cameo did her best to help Rush keep going. He grew weaker from loss of blood the longer they walked. He needed fluids and first-aid. More than that. He needed a doctor, surgery to get the bullet removed. She hoped it hadn't damaged any of his internal organs and that it could be easily taken out.

They'd been trekking through dirt and heat for hours. Rush used the rifle as support for one arm while clutching her shoulder with his free hand. By the position of the sun, she guessed the time to be about three in the afternoon. She was accustomed to this kind of terrain from her work in Australia but even in her top physical condition, she struggled to press on through pain and thirst.

"Shouldn't we have come across a bar or something?" Rush asked.

"We need to stay off road until dark. I'm sure the bastard is awake by now and they're combing the highways for us."

"You're one tough lady."

"Not really. Just stubborn." She laughed a little then coughed from the dryness. "There's a pile of rocks and some brush. We can rest there until dark."

They staggered over to the tiny spot of shade and dropped to the ground, exhausted. Rush stretched out on his back, one hand pressed over the roll of leather on the wound in his side.

"Let me have a look at that." She crawled over to him. Gingerly, she lifted his shirt crusted with dried blood. She examined the wound at his side then eased him over to look for an exit wound. "I think the bullet went straight through, but it made a couple nasty holes." She eased his shirt off then removed her torn shirt and maneuvered it into place to cover both wounds, then she tied both ends tightly. "Hopefully that'll slow down the bleeding. Tonight I'll go and find help."

"I'm not letting you wander off by yourself," he said. "We stick together."

She studied his face, admiring his bravery. "Do you believe in God?"

"Yeah. Why?"

"Rebar has strong faith. We talked about it a few times. He's the most forgiving upright person I've ever known. I'm certain he's praying for us if he survived." A knife sliced through her heart at the thought that he might not have . . .

"Stay with me here, babe. Don't let your mind sink to dark places. We're hurting and I'm on the verge of delirium. You've been a rock all this time. I have never seen a woman fight as hard as you did. And I've never met one hold it together like you did back there."

"Thank you," she said with a grateful smile. "I'm going to pray. That's what Rebar would do."

Rush closed his eyes. Long black lashes touched his cheeks. "I'll pray with you."

Cameo laid a hand over his and bowed her head. She cried out to God for help and forgiveness over killing Joan. Never in her wildest thoughts could she have imagined taking a life, but when faced with terror and imminent peril, she had simply snapped.

After praying, she opened her eyes and noticed Rush had dozed off. *Sleep is nature's healer,* she reminded herself. Quietly, she lay beside him and closed her eyes. The scant shade they'd found offered some relief.

When she opened her eyes next, night had fallen and the sound of footsteps approaching made her bolt upright.

Wow, I must've fallen asleep with him. "Rush," she whispered. "Are you awake?"

"Hm? What is it, baby?" He sounded groggy.

"I hear someone out there walking around. I'm scared."

He pushed to a sitting position and took hold of the rifle. "If it's them, they'll be sorry."

They waited in tense anticipation. Cameo could barely stop

herself from springing up and running but she knew Rush was in no condition to flee. They had no choice but to wait, watch, and possibly defend themselves if necessary. She felt suddenly glad he had grabbed a rifle loaded with ammo.

Endless long minutes passed before the footsteps grew closer and a short silhouette appeared. Cameo hardly dared to breathe as the figure inched closer.

"Hola?" a little girl said from the shadows. "I bring food and water." Her sweet voice sounded almost angelic.

Rush lowered the rifle and laid it beside him.

"Food?" She held out a wicker basket and canteen. "Water?"

"Yes. Come here," Cameo responded.

A beautiful hispanic child, around eight years old, approached. Long black hair draped to her tiny waist. She stared at them with huge dark eyes. A gentle smile touched her perfect lips.

"I walk by here before. You sleep, so I went home and come back with food," she told them in broken English.

The child was absolutely beautiful. She looked like an exquisite well-crafted artist doll. She wore a red gingham skirt, white peasant top, and tan leather moccasins on her small feet. She set the basket before them then handed over the canteen. The water was actually cold.

Rush insisted Cameo drink first. They took turns chugging cool fresh water. Nothing had ever tasted so good.

"You like corn cakes?" the girl asked. "Pears?"

"Oh my gosh, yes." Cameo picked up a flat corn cake and folded a piece of pear inside. "Where are you from, child? What is your name?"

"I live there." She pointed north. "I am Angelica." A look of concern filled her eyes. "You and he hurt." She knelt on the ground and took dirt into her dainty hands, then pulled a cactus leaf from her pocket. After squeezing juice from the leaf, she mixed it with the dirt. "This . . . on pain."

She dabbed the mixture onto Cameo's back with feather-light pats. Cameo exhaled in relief at the little touch of Heaven in this Hell.

"The rest for him," Angelica whispered.

"Thank you," Cameo murmured.

Rush cast Cameo a guarded look but didn't protest when she accepted the girl's medicine and swathed it over both holes then replaced the makeshift bandage.

When she looked up, the girl was gone—just gone. She hadn't heard her walk away or utter another word.

Yet the basket and canteen remained.

"Okay. That was strange," Rush commented.

Cameo didn't say anything right away. She pondered the girl's visit while eating the cakes and fruit. They ate their fill and saved the rest. After lying there a while, Rush's breathing began to sound more relaxed.

"Halo," he murmured.

"I'm here."

"The pain is gone," he told her.

"Really?" She rolled onto her side toward him. "Mine feels better, too."

"Yeah. Amazing. I can take a breath without the stabbing agony."

Cameo looked up into the dark sky, lit only by sparkling stars. "Thank you, Jesus," she whispered. Then she snuggled against Rush with one arm across his bare chest. "I'm glad you're feeling better. Do you mind me being this close? It makes me feel safer."

"Not at all." He wrapped an arm about her shoulders and snuggled her into the curve of his. "You've spent the day worrying over me. How are you doing? Has Rebar seen the scars on your back?"

"Maybe. He probably didn't know how to ask me about

them."

"That man . . . he's your father?"

"So I've been told. My past is complicated."

"I don't know how you endured such a beating."

"The sheer will to defeat him I guess."

"You must be hurting. Is there anything I can do to help?"

She glanced up at his face. He looked down and their eyes met. The intense compassion overflowing in those shadowy depths captured her breath for a split second. Their lips were dangerously close, and despite everything, the faint scent of his cologne and leather jacket pervaded.

He touched his lips to hers. The act was impulsive. She felt no intent in him only the longing to comfort and perhaps receive comfort. They searched each other's eyes. She saw the same conflict in his that she felt in her soul yet the desperate need to feel anything, but agony consumed her.

"Yes," she barely whispered. "Take this horror away even if for just a little while."

He slid his free hand alongside her face. His touch was tender, soothing. Their lips met again in a succession of feathery kisses before he claimed her mouth with his. They sank into a heady exchange of affection laden with desperation.

She knew they would go no farther than kissing, therefore she allowed herself to accept the solace he freely offered. And for an instant, the thought that he could be related to Rebar tugged at her mind again. Why . . . she had no clue, except that for some reason, it almost felt like she was in Rebar's arms . . . almost . . .

Have I become my mother? The question came and went in a flash. She forced everything from her weary mind except the here and now. Time faded, as did her physical pain in the arms of this sweet man who'd risked his life to help a stranger.

The kiss deepened. His breathing swirled around her. His touch revived her. She didn't hold back but channeled all her pain, her sorrow and confusion into their kiss.

We can't go farther, she reminded herself. Her soul was weary. Her spirit battered and bruised.

She eased away from him a few timeless moments later and rested her head on his shoulder. Nothing felt real. She thought about the little girl. "I think she was an angel," Cameo whispered.

"The girl? I doubt angels bring real baskets. But to me, she was a little angel and smart of her to notice that I was bleeding."

"Yeah."

He drew a deep breath and exhaled. "We're gonna be okay, babe. I see why they call you Halo."

CHAPTER SEVEN

"R ush, wake up," Cameo whispered at dawn. "We should get moving before the sun comes up."

His lashes fluttered and he opened his eyes, gazing up at her. "We should eat first."

"Yeah." She unfolded the napkin holding the corn cakes and handed him one. "How are you feeling?"

"Better." He ate the cake and drank a few sips from the little water that was left in the canteen. "How about you?"

"I'll be okay. I'm not the one with a bullet wound." She hoped he wouldn't bring up the kiss. Guilt washed over her.

"You're wounded, too. Your inner wounds run deep, Halo. They, too, can hurt like blazes and they leave scars."

"Scars remind me that the past is real," she told him. "I can never let myself forget as long as that man is alive."

"Why?"

"Because he's been out to get me since day one. Now that he knows I'm back in the States, and that I know his dirty secrets, he'll do anything to stop me from talking. He sent me away when I was five so nobody would know what he did to my mother." She finished her cake and brushed the crumbs off her lap. "We should get going while we're riding this burst of fresh energy. It may not last long." She looked around and found his shirt then pulled it over her head. It felt gross but she couldn't walk about topless, and she didn't want to disturb his wounds by taking her shirt back.

"Wait." He grabbed her hand. "About last night . . ."

She averted her eyes and bit her lip, wondering what he'd

say.

"I hope I didn't make things worse for you."

"No. I get it. We were both desperate and delirious. You took away my pain for just a little while and I'm grateful."

"I don't want you to think I'm that kind of man."

"What kind of man is that?" She still didn't look at him for fear he'd see her conflict.

"A scoundrel who takes advantage of women. I've never gotten involved with a woman during a rescue. I couldn't use her vulnerability for my pleasure."

"I believe you. I'm as much to blame. Now I'm riddled with guilt."

"Don't feel that way, sweetheart. What happened between us was . . . survival. It was only a kiss."

"Is that all it was?" She finally turned to look at him.

He didn't reply straight away but stared back at her with those smoldering black eyes. The feelings he stirred within her troubled her.

"No," he replied softly. "I wanted you the moment I saw you, but I know you're Rebar's girl. I'll never forget what we shared. If things don't work out with Rebar, I won't be far away."

"We've been dating just over a month, and I've already cheated on him. Sort of." She sighed. "I *am* like my mother."

"No. You did nothing wrong. You're not engaged, are you?"

Her brows shot up. "Nooo . . . I'm not even sure I want to get married. Rebar knows that. But I sure can't judge Camille now. She's engaged to Shade but flirts shamelessly with Rebar. They kinda had a thing before I came along."

"Who's Camille?"

"My twin sister. The real Halo. We were separated at birth by that beast. I just found out about her a month ago. A lot has happened since May and it's only July. I was living a peaceful life in Europe until my mother showed up, a mother I had never met. Since then, my life has been a whirlwind."

"I never knew my dad," he admitted. "So I kinda know how you feel. He was killed before I got the chance to meet him. My mom's parents raised me because she traveled a lot."

"Were you raised in the States?" Her curiosity had just gone off the chart.

"Yep. Texas born and raised. Mom was young and attending college when she had me. Since we lived with her parents, I chose to stay when she took a job in another state. I didn't want to leave my friends or school."

"I'm sorry you lost your father. Did your mom tell you who he was?"

Rush nodded. "He was a bigwig oil man in Texas. My mom is beautiful and was a Dallas cheerleader before she decided to move away. That's how she met my dad. He was rich. She was kinda famous. They hooked up. Then she discovered he was married and had sons and another mistress. By that time, my mother was pregnant with me. She wanted no part of his complicated life, but he did set up a trust for me and paid her tuition in addition to sending large checks every month. It was the least he could do for knocking her up and ending her career as a cheerleader."

Cameo withheld a gasp. His story was so much like Rebar's she knew her instincts had been right on target. This man had to be the son of Tassos and there was a third brother! She sat back on her knees, gazing at him in utter shock.

"Are you okay?" he asked, reaching for her. "You look like you've seen a ghost."

"Your father . . . do you know his name?"

Rush scrunched his brows as if it was a silly question. "Yeah, babe. Why?"

"Just that," she swallowed hard. "Your story sounds uncannily familiar."

"How so?"

"I may know your brothers."

His eyes widened and brows lifted. "Nah. Surely, I'd have met them by now. My mom would've known them . . . maybe. Maybe not . . ." He paused in thought. "No I guess not. She never asked about his wife or the other mistress. She didn't want to know about them. Geez, I guess I have two half-brothers floating around out there somewhere. I never gave it much thought or tried to find them. They probably don't know about me either. Seems my father got around."

"Just a little," she scoffed. "What was his name?"

"Tassos . . . Tassos Damocles."

"Oh. My. Gosh." Her mouth dropped open.

"What? What? You know him?" He cast her a panicked look. "We're not related, are we?"

"No, no." She shook her head. "But I do know your brothers . . . one of them intimately. Wait. You've known Chamber a long time, right?"

Concern creased his brow. "Is *he* my brother?"

"Not that I know of but I'm wondering why he never told you. He's known them for years. Surely he put the last names together."

"What last names? You're talking in circles, babe."

"Damocles. Not exactly a common surname. Why wouldn't Chamber tell you about your brothers' last names?"

"Because that's not my last name," Rush replied. "I never wanted the man's name. He cheated on his wife with two other women, maybe more. My last name is Levvy. It's my mother's maiden name. She gave it to me at birth and I never wanted to change it for a father I would never meet."

"Wow . . . this is mind-blowing." She sat there, dumbfounded, at a loss for words. "I'm so sorry that I dropped this on you."

"What? That I have two brothers somewhere? I already

knew that. Just didn't try to find them. I'm sure there are a lot of my half-siblings roaming around unaware of each other."

"But yours are right here. Shade and Rebar Damocles." She dropped her head in her hands. "I've just kissed my boyfriend's brother. I'm no better than Camille or my mom."

"Hey . . ." He murmured, lifting her chin with a tender touch so that their eyes met. "I'm not a bad guy. I knew nothing about my brothers. You could've done worse."

She couldn't withhold a light laugh. "I'm sorry. I didn't mean it that way. I came down on my sister for being in love with Rebar while she's engaged to Shade. Then what do I do?"

"No disrespect intended, but if Rebar was meeting all your needs, you'd never have been tempted to return the kiss. There must be something about your relationship with him that makes you vulnerable. I've met hundreds of women and learned to read them well."

She pondered his words and realized he was right. "Camille," she said softly.

"You said they had a fling?"

"A thing. They had a *thing* not a fling. He has some deep connection with her because of the PTSD. I'm still not sure she's over him or that she even wants to marry Shade. We didn't exactly get off to a good start since our first meeting."

"You and your twin are in love with two brothers. And those two guys are my half-brothers?" He shook his head. "Small weird world."

"Shade and Rebar are half-brothers, too. Apparently, according to my mother, Camille and I have different fathers, but I find that impossible to believe. I've never heard of identical twins sired by two men. But my stubborn sister refuses to have a DNA test. She denies that the General could be her sire, too. Can't say I blame her."

They sat quietly for a bit, processing the facts. A flood of emotions deluged Cameo. She almost wished she'd never returned to the States with her mother. She did love Rebar, but Rush was right. Camille was an invisible barrier between them that popped up every now and then without warning.

She thought about how she'd been living in her twin's shadow the past month. Everyone who met them compared her to Camille. Her sister was in tight with Shade's crew and seemed to have most of them wrapped around her pretty little finger.

Though Rebar insisted he no longer had feelings for Camille, the subtle hints of lingering affection rose to the surface now and then. She supposed Rebar hadn't worried about sharing his battle with PTSD with Camille because they understood each other, and he'd helped her cope with hers.

"Maybe the right thing to do is to let go," she finally said.

He turned those gorgeous eyes toward her. "Of what?"

"Everything. My presence caused so much trouble in the troop. If I bow out now, there's time for them to find their way back to each other."

"Don't make any decisions right now. You're not in a good state of mind."

"I'm trying too hard. I even traded my Shelby for a Gran Sport. I didn't think much of it when I did it, but maybe I was subconsciously trying to create a bond with Rebar that Camille doesn't have." She sighed despondently. "I'm such a mess."

"How'd you and he meet anyway?"

"He thought I was Camille and followed me. Then I smashed up his car because they had me cornered. He was persistent and I agreed to a date with him. He's a true sweetheart and deserves the right woman. But maybe that woman isn't me. Maybe he's trying too hard, too." She laughed a little. "Hell, maybe we're all trying too hard. Camille's trying to love Shade, Rebar's trying to love me, and I'm . . ."

"You're what?" His eyes searched hers.

"I'm just running scared."

"Well, babe. I don't know Camille. Never met her. And I'm not fired up about knowing my brothers either. So if we could just keep this on the downlow I'd appreciate it."

"You don't want them to know you're their brother?"

"No. I have nothing in common with them. From what I've heard about Shade, I doubt we'd get along. I like Rebar, which is why he should never know. We could never be friends."

"Why?"

He leaned toward her, taking her face between gentle hands. "Because I'm gonna take his woman." The sensual sway in his voice, the hot expression in his eyes, left her speechless. He brushed his lips over hers, letting his tongue flick between them.

She gasped at his bold declaration and unexpected aggression. He was daring and raw, a true rebel and fearless hero. Her emotions swirled as he kissed her long and deep.

Maybe Malika wasn't the only one needing rescuing, she thought, then let Rush sweep her worries away once more.

Rebar couldn't hide his frustration over having to wait a whole day for the bikes to be repaired. The crash was worse than they initially thought, and the mechanic had to call another shop for parts. He wondered how Cameo was holding up and where the General had taken her.

Chamber walked up from behind. "Bikes are almost ready. Any idea which way to start our search?"

"No. I thought maybe he'd take her back to his mansion but that seems too easy. I don't know the man. I've no idea how he thinks."

"But I do," a woman said from the side entrance as the door swung open.

In strutted a tall, slender, stunning vixen with long raven black hair and the most seductive doe eyes he'd ever seen. She was dressed in moccasins, tan leggings and a fringed buckskin dress that hung just past her hips.

Every man in the garage stopped to gawk. Tools clanked on the floor. Machines ground to a halt. Her unexpected presence emanated power and sexuality at its highest.

"You must be Malika," Rebar concluded.

She gave a curt nod and smiled slightly.

Before she said a word, another woman came running into the garage past Malika and straight to Rebar. She flung her arms around him.

"When I heard about the accident, I had to come. Nothing could've stopped me. Are you all right? I heard there was shooting, and all the guys were down. Are you okay?" Camille's words came out in an airy rush.

"Camille! What are you doing here? Did the troop come to help?"

She shook her head sadly. "No. I'm sorry. It's just me and my . . . me and Malika."

"You reconciled with your mother?" He was shocked and pleased.

"For now," she replied. "We'll see how things go. But I had to come when she said you were hurt."

"What about Shade?" Rebar glanced toward the doorway.

"No. He was furious when Malika showed up at the house with Shook. They told us what happened. How you and some group called Ricochet rescued her from the General. We followed Shook down in my car. Malika told me everything, Rebar, everything."

"So you believe your sister now?" His hope rose for healing between them.

"Yes. Where is she? I want to apologize for the way I treated her."

Rebar forced his emotions back. "They took her. Missy, Joan, and that bastard shot Rush. Then Missy used a stun gun on the rest of us while her two cohorts took Cameo and Rush."

"Oh no. This is awful."

At that moment, Shook sauntered into the garage. He went to his comrades first, then all of them meandered over to join the women. He introduced everyone to Malika. She had seemingly won Shook over somewhere between Raton and Denver.

"We were going to start searching yesterday but the bikes weren't ready," Rebar told the new arrivals.

"Good thing," Malika said in a voice that could melt glaciers. "You'd be chasing your tails."

Rebar glanced at Shook. "You trust her?"

"Yeah. She hasn't left my side since I put her on my bike the other night. Shade was wrong about everything."

"How do we find them?" Rebar asked her.

"The General took her back to his mansion. He always retreats to home base when a mission fails. I don't know how you found us, but I'm impressed. And all this time I thought Shade was the right man for my Camille. I underestimated you, Rebar Damocles. I thought you were just one of Shade's puppets."

Her remark made him feel awkward. *Did she actually just imply that I belong with Camille?* Seeing Camille again, feeling her hug the stuffing out of him, brought back a surge of buried feelings he thought were gone.

Camille stepped back and looked him over. "Oh my, look at you. You're all scraped up and bruised." She ran her hands lightly up his arms. "Any serious injuries? I haven't forgotten my nursing skills."

"Everyone here is okay. Banged up, but nothing serious. We're not sure about Rush, though. He was bleeding and unconscious when they dragged him away."

"We'll find your friend," she assured him.

He noticed her left hand no longer wore a ring. "What's going on with you and Shade? I'm surprised he let you come."

"He didn't." She shifted her weight uneasily. "We broke up."

"You did?"

"He refused to believe the General could do any wrong, even after everything Shook and Malika told him. When I said I was going with them to help, he told me if I did, that it was over. That no woman of his would be so foolish. So, I threw the ring at him, and walked out."

Rebar digested her words. His mind reeled. Here stood the woman he'd wanted since the day they met, yet he was in love with her twin. Or was he? Confusion settled over him like a cold wet blanket. He realized his feelings for Camille hadn't gone away as he'd thought. Seeing her. Hearing her caring voice. Feeling her touch and innate ability to nurture reminded him of why he'd fallen so hard for her in the first place.

However, he was never free to explore those feelings because Shade had claimed her first.

She and Cameo were polar opposites. Cameo was tough, independent, and dangerously alluring—much like her mother. Camille on the other hand possessed a nurturing side toward him that made him feel safe. They'd both shared their struggles with PTSD. He'd never worried that it would scare her. They did have a connection that went beyond his logic.

Had he been trying too hard all this time to bury his feelings for Camille and love her twin the same way? No. He did love Cameo, but differently. Their relationship was edgy and unpredictable. They had a lot in common such as their taste in cars, food, and combat.

Maybe we're too much alike.

"We have to rescue your sister and Rush," he said,

diverting the conversation away from her breakup with Shade.

Camille pulled him off to the side. "I'm free now, Rebar. Are you engaged to my sister yet or just dating?"

"Our relationship has grown quite close, but it's only been a little more than a month. We're not engaged."

"Then there's still time for us to explore our feelings for each other. I always thought you felt something for me. Was I wrong?"

"No. You weren't wrong. But I'm in a relationship now. I can't just dump Cameo to run off with her sister. That would be cruel."

"Do you love each other?"

"Yes."

"It's been a bumpy road, though, hasn't it?"

She read him too well. Or perhaps she was merely seeing his fatigue. Either way, she was right.

"She keeps life interesting," he murmured.

"You don't need more stress. I know how you love your quiet time at the lodge. She's brought so much chaos to your life."

"You're being a naughty sister." He wagged a finger at her. "Trying to steal her man."

"No. I'm trying to save her man from making a huge mistake. Malika and I talked a lot during the four-hour drive down here. She helped me understand Cameo who is a lot like her."

Rebar couldn't deny she made valid points any more than he could hide how he felt about her. He was certain she could see it in his eyes.

"Can we talk about this later? Right now, your sister needs help. You don't know her story or how we fought our way out of the mansion together. Everything's not black and white."

Camille backed down gracefully. "I'm sorry. You're right. I don't mean to sound cold but I'm just so happy to see you. I couldn't wait to tell you that I'm free." She caught him off guard by laying an intensely affectionate kiss on his lips.

He eased back from the kiss. "Whoa, kitten. You're making assumptions."

"I've known you much longer than she has. I just wanted to let you know where I stand." She reached up and touched his face as only she could do.

He recalled their many evenings sitting on the porch talking, laughing — it was so easy being with her. Still, he couldn't go there now. His girlfriend was in serious trouble. He led Camille back to the others.

"Are the bikes ready yet?"

Chamber shot him a probing look. "Yeah. You okay?"

"I don't know, man. My head's a mess."

"You shouldn't be driving then."

"I can drive his car," Camille piped up.

"Not a good idea," Chamber told her. "Drive yours. Take Malika with you. I can leave my bike here and drive his car."

"Nobody's driving my car," Rebar snapped. "I'll be fine. Actually, it's probably what I need most right now . . . time alone in my car to straighten out my head, and I don't mean in a physical way. Let's go find our friends."

Malika sauntered over to him and draped one arm casually over his shoulder. "Torn between my daughters, young man?"

He stared back into her entrancing eyes. "Does that please you?"

A mischievous grin curved her flawlessly red-painted lips. "Of course. Men are the enemy until they are tamed."

"Is that what you sent Cameo out to do? Tame me?"

"You made the decision to pursue her. Nobody pushed you off the cliff." She leaned in closer, so close he could smell her exotic perfume. "Cameo is stronger than Camille. She can't be bought, bribed, blackmailed, or defeated. Camille on the other hand is a follower, a nurturing fragile girl. Both of my daughters are smitten with you. The question is, which one can you handle? The wildcat or the kitten?" Her lips brushed his ear as she whispered, "think about that while riding *alone* in your hot car."

Rebar watched her sashay back to Shook, who slipped an arm around her slender waist. He didn't know Shook's age but in a strange way, he and Malika fit.

"Looks like Shook and Malika hit it off." Chamber gave Rebar a playful nudge.

"Yeah . . ." Rebar dipped one brow. "How old is Shook anyway?"

"Just turned fifty. He's the old man of our group. Rush is the baby at only forty-one. The rest of us fall in between."

"Malika looks young for her age," Rebar stated. "I'm surprised she didn't make a play for Shade."

"What makes you say that?"

Rebar shrugged. "A few remarks made by Cameo and Shade."

"She's only fifty-seven, guys," Camille interrupted. "She got pregnant with us at sixteen."

Rebar couldn't stop watching Malika flirt with Shook. Suddenly his entire world felt like a foreign land. Camille was back and openly pursuing him. A guy he'd just met was hooking up with the renowned Malika before his very eyes. He didn't imagine Shade would fall for the seductress since he'd seen her kill Dale.

At the moment, nothing made sense.

What he wanted was to find Cameo, and retreat to his lodge for months. Though he was grateful for Ricochet's help, the rescue had gone bad, and his girl got caught in the fray. He couldn't bear the thought of her suffering after all they'd shared.

Camille's one-eighty felt confusing. Riding with Chamber's friends had taken him out of his comfort zone. He prayed Rush had more self-control than Shook and hadn't put the moves on Cameo. He doubted a wounded man in their predicament would have enough strength to pursue a woman.

Still, it seemed with these Parker women, anything was possible. A foreboding feeling crept over him. Was he headed for heartbreak? Malika didn't seem worse for wear considering what she'd just endured. The woman was pure fire and ice. She did not look or behave like a victim of abuse. Nor did she exhibit a hint of trauma.

"You're tripping," Chamber muttered from his side. "What's going on in that busy brain of yours?"

"That I'm in over my head."

"Let's ride then. Everyone's ready." Chamber gave him a friendly slap on the back. "Shouldn't take long to find them with all of us going in. We've got a three-hour drive down to his mansion in Santa Fe. The plan is to surround the estate and wait till dark then sneak in and get them out."

"That's if they're still there," Rebar stated. "You don't know Cameo. She's a fighter."

Concern shadowed Chamber's face. "Then let's pray, for her sake, she decided to stay put and wait for help this time. You wanna lead out since you've been to the mansion before?"

"Yeah, sure."

Everyone straddled their Harleys. Rebar slid behind the wheel of his Gran Sport—the only place that felt like home right now.

He watched Malika kiss Shook before gracefully getting into the passenger seat of Camille's Shelby. Something about Camille's mother gnawed at his gut yet he couldn't discern what.

Was it her arrogance?

Her bewitching beauty?

Or was it the way she'd taunted him regarding her daughters?

He turned the key and embraced the sound of his Stage One engine firing up. For the next three hours he'd crank the stereo and lose himself in the power growling through the dual exhaust.

A late day sun glinted off the gleaming black paint of his hood when the car rumbled from the garage. He drew a deep breath and forced all paranoid thoughts from his mind.

Santa Fe was practically a straight shot down Interstate 25. He saw Chamber, Moss, and Levi in his rearview mirror on his tail. Camille's white Shelby followed with Shook bringing up the rear.

Soon. Very soon, Cameo would be safely back in his arms and in his car. Then he could retreat to his lodge and leave this madness behind. He just hoped Cameo would be content with her mother's freedom and avoid future entanglements in any revenge plots Malika had in mind.

Rebar doubted very much that this was the end of Malika's drama. She saw men as the enemy and was probably already devising another plan to accomplish her vendetta against the General.

Now that she had both of her daughters together, would she enlist their help? Would the three of them bond over a common enemy and set out to destroy the man who had kept them apart for decades?

The seductress seemed hellbent on revenge at any cost.

Perhaps this was the gnawing feeling he felt — that Malika's long-awaited reunion with both twins was only the beginning of a new chapter.

Read what happens next in Feather Blue 5!

ABOUT THE AUTHOR

Shiloh is a bookworm who grew into an author. Writing has been a way of life for her since grade school. She majored in English, graduated and eventually found success with a few good publishers. January 1, 2016 Shiloh officially went Indie. In her words, "The only time I'm truly free is when I'm writing."

As a survivor of hardship and chronic disease, she takes one day at a time and treasures the simple things in life. Shiloh is a Christian, loves animals and practices being kind and generous every day.

Her achievements include The Golden Wings Award for her debut novel The Satellite, the UK Nobel Pin and Editor's Choice Award for her poem The Lonely Man, numerous 5 Star Reviews from Fallen Angels Reviews, InD'tale Magazine, and other professional reviewers for novels published under former pen names.

Her novel Forever in Darkness became a finalist in the 2017 RONE Awards.

Her novel *Chained Reaction* earned her third 5 Star Crowned Heart Review and a nomination for the RONE 2021 Awards.

Writing stories you'll live in!

www.SusanZoeBella.com